# Looking Further Backward

*Arthur Dudley Vinton*

# Contents

**LOOKING FURTHER BACKWARD.**

Being a Series of

**LECTURES**

Delivered to the Freshman Class

at

*SHAWMUT COLLEGE,*


By PROFESSOR WON LUNG LI,

(Successor of Prof. Julian West),


MANDARIN OF THE SECOND RANK OF THE GOLDEN DRAGON

AND CHIEF OF THE HISTORICAL SECTIONS

OF THE COLLEGES IN THE NORTH-EASTERN

DIVISION OF THE CHINESE PROVINCE

OF NORTH AMERICA,

NOW FOR THE FIRST TIME,

COLLECTED, EDITED, AND CONDENSED.


BY **ARTHUR DUDLEY VINTON.**

——

ALBANY BOOK COMPANY

36 STATE STREET

ALBANY, N.Y.,

1890

## Dedication

TO

*MOSES TAYLOR PYNE*,

A WISE COUNSELLOR, A TRUE FRIEND

AND A NOBLE MAN,

THIS BOOK

IS

*DEDICATED*

AS A TOKEN OF THE

ESTEEM, HONOR AND ADMIRATION

WITH WHICH HE IS REGARDED BY ALL WHO KNOW HIM,

AND ESPECIALLY

BY

THE AUTHOR.

# Preface

One of the wonders of the age has been the remarkable success of Edward Bellamy's novel *Looking Backward*. The reason for this is not hard to guess. The majority of the thinking portion of the community found in this book an echo of their own thought. In a simple and attractive way it set before the public mind the horrible iniquity of the present organization, of society. The comparison of our social system to a coach whereon a few persons sit in indolence, while the vast majority, driven by hunger, toil at the ropes and drag the coach along, has appealed to every honest mind by its truthfulness. A slavery, worse than that which made a nation rise to free the blacks, has risen with a fungus growth and made the rich man and the poor man enemies. Corrupt judges on the bench and partisan grand juries in the precincts of the courts have made one law for the rich and another for the poor. Poverty has become a synonym for dishonor. The possession of money is alone the one source of respect upon earth and assurance of reward in heaven.

The enormous growth of private fortunes and the organization of capital by great corporations have been so sudden, and have so altered our social system from vrhat it was thirty years ago, that men are bewildered at the change. The elder men cannot realize it. It is the younger men alone who see that the chains and shackles which a bloody war struck from the African, are being rivetted anew upon the laboring man. They alone see that the existence of great private fortunes is a menace to the welfare of the State, and that (with a few honorable exceptions) their possessors are public enemies.

In their bewilderment at the new state of affairs, men have asked themselves the old question, "What shall we do to be saved ?" And it is because Edward Bellamy in *Looking Backward* and Lawrence Gronlund in *The Co-operative Commonwealth*, have attempted to answer this question, that their books have received so much attention. The benefit which these books have done is very great; but the Utopian schemes which they recommend as remedies for the evils which exist to-day are fraught with danger.

Whatever promises to regenerate mankind or better the chances for life, liberty and happiness, I am heartily in favor of. But a false guide is worse than no guide, and a wrong solution of a great human problem is worse than no solution; and, therefore, I have endeavored in the following story, to point out wherein the Bellamy Nationalism woiJd prove disastrously weak.

Fortunately in these United States, we have no need to appeal to violence, nor to change our form of government to accomplish any desired reform. Theoretically and legally, our government is of the people and from the people, and laws reforming the present abominable oiganization of society can be passed whenever the people are sufficiently enlightened to see the wisdom of enacting them. The story has been so favorably and publicly criticised while in manuscript, that I am encouraged to hope it may serve a good purpose in print.

Arthur Dudley Vinton.
New York, 1890.

## Chapter 1 *LECTURE I.*

HISTORICAL SECTION, SHAWMUT COLLEGE,

*Boston, A. D. 2023,*

and in the Year of the Great Dragon, 7942.

Won Lung Li, *Professor of History*,
To the American Barbarians:

I come before you as a stranger. I am born of a race that the race you are born of has for centuries been trained to think of as an inferior race.

I have no doubt that there may be some persons among you who look upon me not only as a man of alien race, but as an instructor placed over you by the force of arms, a director of your thought, a guide to your historical studies, forced upon you by the physical supremacy of an alien nation.

I recognize that such thoughts may be entertained by you. I would not even blame you for entertaining them. I approach my task with diffidence as great as your reluctance to be instructed by me can be. The tongue I speak to you in is not my own tongue. I must invite your attention to events which you must necessarily feel a sense of humiliation in considering, since they evidence the foolishness of your ancestors, and the strange infatuation for impracticable ideas that dominated your immediate progenitors. I must narrate to you a history that you can take little pride in. Mine is the unpleasant task to dwell with you upon the causes that led to what many of you consider your degradation. Having thus besought your favor, I begin the first of those lectures which, as Professor of History in Shawmut College, it is my duty to deliver and your duty to attend.

Twenty-three years ago, in the year 2000, according to your former method of calculating from the birth of Jesus Christ, one Julian West, who then occupied the chair of history, now occupied by me, wrote a book which he called *Looking Backward*[1] This book you have all perused in your earlier historical studies; and you are all somewhat familiar with the condition of society which it purported to describe. I will not, therefore, dwell upon it for any length of time, though some reference to it is necessary, as I propose in my lectures to you, to continue the history of your country from the period at which Professor West stops to the present day.

You will remember that Professor West, in his book, gave many of his own sensations, but few of his own impressions or observations as to the social conditions which surrounded him on his awakening from his strange sleep. He confined himself to repeating the opinions and remarks of a certain garrulous old gentleman, called Dr. Leete. Your previous studies have also informed you that this gentleman took a most optimistic and favorable view of his own times, and, especially, of the remarkable system of government under which your parents then suffered.

Before proceeding to the direct study of the events of the last quarter century, it is necessary that you should understand some, at least, of the defects of that extraordinary system of government, because it was through those defects that the father of our present reigning Emperor, was enabled to endow you with the glorious civilization of China, and to give to you, even against the will of your barbarian progenitors, our present happy system of government. These defects it is my purpose to point out to you — not always in my own words, however, but often in the words of Professor West. I copy his criticism of them from manuscripts, in his own handwriting, found among his baggage after the second batlie of Lake Erie, where, as you know, he fell at the head of the regiment which he had raised from the graduates of the Historical Section of Shawmut College. He writes :

" Dr. Leete was a very talkative old gentleman, whose explanations were quite interesting for a while, but after a little time, he began to tell his stories over and over again and insisted on explaining every thing to me a second and third time; so I made tip my mind that it was decidedly my duty to be idle no longer, but to at once assume my professorship at Shawmut College. In repeated interviews with my host I made this quite plain. Li a little while, therefore, I was installed in my professorship, much to Dr. Leete's regret, for he had probably never before had so good a listener as I had been.

" My marriage with Edith, soon followed.

" At first, when I had been but recently awakened, every thing was so strange to me that I felt confused and bewildered.

The only sensation that I was capable of, was surprise. The analytical powers of my mind were in a state of abeyance. But, after I had become more familiar with the society into which the strange sequence of phenomenal events had cast me, I began to see that Dr. Leete had pictured things in altogether too roseate a light. Human nature, I found, was much the same as it had been a century ago. There were now, as then, people who thought that the existing state of affairs was the best that could be devised; but there were many, now, as then, who were discontented with their condition in life, and ready to welcome any change. Human ambition was as actiye now as it had been then, only it ran in different channels. The spirit of acquisitiveness, the desire of gain, manifested itself in more than one of the men whom I was thrown into contact with. It did not, to be sure, show itself in the desire to accumulate money, for two generations had had no use for money, and could have no practical knowledge of the superiority which the possession of great riches gave to men of my time. But I was made sharp-sighted by an experience which none now living, except myself, has had, and I could see that the desire to accumulate property was still with many men a ruling motive, which manifested itself in many ways. I saw, moreover, that demagoguery and corruption[2] were not words having only in historical significance, as Dr. Leete would have had me believe, but that favoritism was rank in all branches of the public service, that officials were constantly being impeached for it —the men for giving the prettier women advantage over those who were homelier, while the women took fancies to men, and made distinctions in their favor. From my present observations, I am inclined to think that the women are far more given to this vice of favoritism than the men are.

" The inheritance of property[3] was still permitted; and this, allowyig the accumulation of valuable goods and chattels, was a continual source of inequality—though Dr. Leete had told me to the contrary. I found that one family (by the name of Bassett) in Boston had gradually become possessed of. the masterpieces of American artists, while another (the Hayes family) was envied for its wonderful collection of gold and silver ornaments. The price of jewels, too, had risen enormously above what it had been in my day, owing probably to the fact that these were especially desirable as heirlooms, since they were intrinsically beautiful in themselves, and capable of being stored in such small compass that their possession was no burden.


" I found, also, that the grading and re-grading system,[4] which Dr. Leete had described to me as meeting with universal approval, was a standing grievance to every one who did not rise at all and to many who rose, as they thought, too slowly; and was prolific in engendering discontent and envy."

Thus far we have the testimony of Professor West as to the most apparent faults of what we now call the old order of society. He left behind him other writings than that from which I have just quoted, and these writings (among them, a diary of the events which he took part in) I shall have occasion to quote from later on. After his death at the battle of Lake Erie, his papers were taken possession of by the Chinese authorities, and upon my appointment to this professorship at Shawmut College, were delivered to me.

Your previous studies will have told you what professor West mentions in his book, that the Nationalist idea of government prevailed at the opening of this century, in all of Europe, all of North America and in the greater part of South America,[5] I do not think that he mentions that the Nationalistic notions also prevailed to an extent in India and Russian Asia; nor that the Nationalists of Great Britain had secured a quiet government only after the complete deportation of all the Irish to Australia — which since that day has been in a continued state of anarchy. China alone of all the principal nations upon the globe had retained her ancient civilization and form of government. It is fortunate for the world that she did so.

So far, what I have had to say to you has been in the nature of an introduction. Let me now recite the events that brought about the fall of the Nationalistic system. Most of these events your previous studies have already made you acquainted with, but it is my purpose to so recite them that you can see the cause and effect of each and the relation which one bears to the others.

We learn from our books of history that the French have always been a fickle nation, fond of change, eager in the pursuit of ideas. They were the first to follow the example of the United States and adopt the Nationalist idea of government. They were first also to depart from that idea.

On the 6th of January, A. D. 2012, a riot broke out at Marseilles, the occasion being the public announcement of orders from the government to curtail the manufacture of toys. For many years France had been the toy-shop of the world and Paris had been the principal manufacturer and sales-agent of playthings; but in the preceding decade Marseilles had rivalled the industrial importance of Paris, and much jealousy and ill-feeling had in consequence been engendered between the two cities. When the orders from the central government were promulgated, it was at once believed by the Marseillais that the Parisians had secured their passage; and the occasion was used as a pretext to begin a revolution which we, in the light of subsequent events, and with the knowledge we now possess, have every reason to believe had been carefully arranged beforehand.

I stood once on the slope of Tung-nan, one of the great mountain ranges of my mother country. I was well up toward the summit, and with my guides had halted for a little while to rest. Sitting on a projecting crag, far above the tree line, I, in an idle mood, cast upon the loose scoriae below a fragment of rock that had lain beside me. The missile did work that I had not contemplated. It struck the volcanic debris and rolled slowly downward ; and, as it went, other stones followed it, and they in turn dislodged other stones, until at length an avalanche roared down the mountain side beneath me. The idle casting of a stone had set huge fragments of rocks descending earthward. Trifles are sometimes pregnant ol great things. Great oaks from little acorns grow. The world is changed because a stone is thrown.

When you were at school you learned dates and names, events and, sometimes, results of events. But in my lectures to you I shall endeavor to direct your attention, not only to events and to results, but also to causes; because until yon know the cause you cannot rightly measure the result. The study of causes enables us better to appreciate results; it greatly broadens the scope of our knowledge, and greatly develops the reasoning powers of our mind. When once we have learned that a certain result will follow given causes, we have added to the suin of human knowledge. I would, therefore, impress upon your minds now, at the outset of our historical studies, the importance of seeking for the causes that led in the past to those social changes which have marked the rise or decadence of nations; and especially of those causes which immediately resulted in the fall of the Nationalistic system of government. If yoii would understand history — if you would know the shoals and quicksands that have once before threatened disaster to the ship of state — so that the dangers of past years may warn you what currents of thought and channels of action it is dangerous to follow, you must bring to the accomplishment of that understanding three qualities of mind: you must be students, gathering facts from the records of past ages, creating nothing, only bringing out what is; you must be philosophers, deducing by sound processes of reasoning, by trustworthy comparisons and impartial analyses, general principles which may be safely followed; and you must be statesmen to comprehend the purposes and opinions of masses of men, to observe and measure with accuracy the instrumentalities by which parties or organizations have sought to carry out their principles, and to render their policies acceptable or beneficial to the nation. It was because your ancestors did not understand history that they failed to be forewarned by its obvious teachings, or to appreciate the omens that foretold the coming catastrophe.

Chief among such warnings was the Revolution in France. It was the stone which set the avalanche in motion. It was the first of the series of events which have changed the form of your government; and, therefore, I shall in my next lecture ask you to consider it with some minuteness.

## Chapter 2 *LECTURE II.*

At the time that the Marseillais revolted, France was under the Nationalistic system of government. There were no police and no regular army, and the government had no machinery to quell the disorder that arose. To be sure the superintendents of the other trades in Marseilles, acting under telegraphic instructions from the Central Council at Paris, attempted to organize the employees of those trades into restraining forces; but as these employees sympathized with the rioters they exercised no restraint upon the disorder, so that the authorities at Paris found themselves obliged to recruit a force from the Parisians, and to dispatch this force to Marseilles. This was, as your histories will tell you, the work of several days, and the delay gave the Marseillais time to organize into a regular military force.

This rebellion brought to light two defects in the Nationalist form of government. First, the lack of secrecy in the deliberations of those high in office; and second, the peril which every government must be in when it has failed to maintain a standing army large enough to enforce order, or to do police duty in times of local rebellion or disturbance. Because there had been no war for a century, the Nationalists had looked upon war as an impossibility; military science had been forgotten, and there had been no manufacture of munitions of war. Hence now, when there was an imperative need of an army, the only military force which the French government could put into the field was no better than an undisciplined mob armed with antiquated weapons which had been manufactured more than a century before. We have one of these identical weapons among the curiosities in the museum of Shawmut College; it was intended to be discharged with " powder " — a somewhat bulky material, the principal ingredients of which were charcoal, sulphur and saltpetre. This nondescript army was enlisted, equipped and forwarded by rail to within a few miles of Marseilles, about a fortnight after the rioting first broke out. This delay gave the revolutionists time to mature their plans.

Happily I am in position to throw new light upon the subject of this French Revolution. About two years previous to its outbreak, I had been appointed to a responsible position in the Chinese Bureau of Foreign Intelligence, and with a view of acquiring knowledge which would fit me for the duties of that position, I had spent the preceding year and six months in Europe and North America.

Though the policy of China, ever since the Nationalistic systein of government was generally adopted, had- been to render more strict our ancient policy of non-intercourse with foreign nations, our rulers had none the less recognized the importance of knowing accurately and intimately exactly what foreign governments were doing. Our Bureau of Foreign Intelligence was, therefore, considered by our statesmen as one of the most important departments of the government, and was maintained most liberally and admirably. Subsequent events proved that our statesmen had acted most wisely.

We, in China, had long seen the signs of a disintegration of the Nationalistic governments, although your philosophers and rulers appeared lamentably blind to them. The French Revolution had not surprised us. We not only foresaw it, but we aided it. The men, who, during the, fortnight that the Paris government was practically paralyzed, organized and drilled the

Marseillais, had visited China and had had the benefit of instruction in our military schools. The self-supplying airguns, with which the Marseillais were armed, were manufactured in China and had been secretly shipped to France.in anticipation of this very uprising. Indeed, there is now no harm in saying that the revolutionary movement in France was fomented, aided and abetted by China.

Your school-books have already told you how the Marseillais met and defeated the government troops — that mockery of an army. You know how one success followed another and how the Nationalistic government melted before the armies of the new rulers as the snow melts beneath the rays of the April sun. You know, too, what general distress followed among the people, who had been so long accustomed to rely upon government for labor and support that they were too bewildered to labor individually and too helpless to support life by their individual resources. You know, too, how gladly they welcomed the establishment of the Empire and the reorganization of society on the feudal basis with modifications derived from the Chinese system of government. You know all this. It was part of your earlier historical studies. Therefore, I will not dwell upon it now.

But while, as I have said, we in China were not surprised at the French Revolution nor at its success, we were surprised, and very greatly surprised, that the United States were so little warned by it. That the people were blind was not astonishing, since all the news that they received was what the government gave them in daily bulletins, usually very meagre; and to adversely criticise Nationalism or to point out its many weaknesses, at home or abroad, was treason and promptly punished as such. I repeat, that we in China were not surprised that the people of the United States took no note of the danger that might threaten them; but that their rulers were not warned was to us indeed astonishing.

I do not think that your school histories impart the information that after the establishment of the French Empire, France became practically a dependency of China and annually paid to China a tribute of many million taels. Such, however, was the fact— and it is a fact that must be remembered in considering the subsequent events that took place during the war between the United States and China.

The declaration, by China, of war against the United States undoubtedly took the latter nation by surprise. I quote, on this subject, from Professor Julian West's diary.

He says, under date of September 29th, 2020:

" We arrived in town this morning, all well but all sorry that our summer vacation in the Adiron-dacks has ended. Edith has been very busy all day getting the house in order."

Under date of September 30th, he writes :

" We returned home last night, too late for me to complete the entries of yesterday's happenings under their proper date. I, therefore, write them down to-day. We dined last night with the Berrians (descendants of the novelist). I was afraid that Edith was too tired to go out after her day's travel and household labors, and suggested, when we received the invitation, that we send a regret and spend the evening quietly at home — but she would have none of my suggestions, so we went. On our way we noticed that the streets seemed more full of people than usual; but as there was no appearance of excitement, it did not occur to us that any thing unusual had called the people from their houses. It was not until we were seated at the dinner table and my host had asked me what I thought of the news, and I had answered that, having just returned to town, I knew of no news of importance, that I learned that China had declared war against us.

" The news was a surprise to me for I had never surmised that what few relations we had with China were otherwise than friendly. I was inclined to be alarmed at it also, but Edith and the Berrians were so calm, and so confident that our rulers at Washington would take all necessary measures of offense and defense, that I was almost assured that my alarm was groundless. The news, however, served as a topic of conversation during dinner and afterward, and I was obliged to recall what little I knew about our relations with China in the nineteenth century. Unfortunately this was not a subject to which I had given attention, and I was astonished at my ignorance of it.

" As we went home we took occasion to pass by one of the public bulletin boards on which the news is printed by the government; but the announcement there simply stated that war had been declared, that the President was in consultation with the Generals of the several great guilds, and that further information would be furnished to-morrow. This was not very satisfactory to me, and I so expressed myself to Edith as we walked homeward, telling her also, as well as I was able, how the news would have been promulgated and received in my day; how the news-boys would have been crying extra editions of the newspapers through the streets; how the city would have been awake all the night; how the regular army would be hurrying east and west to man the coast defenses, and every navy yard hard at work. She listened with apparent interest to my descriptions and advised me to embody them in a lecture; but she was so confident that it was the duty of the officials at Washington to attend to all affairs of national defense, that I could not get her to show the slightest interest in anticipating what their action would be. Her reliance upon these officials and her confidence in their wisdom seemed to be shared by the Bostonians generally, for, though it was not midnight when we were returning, the city was as quiet and the streets as deserted as on a Sunday night.

" Leete[6] was sitting up for us on our return. We naturally expressed surprise that he was not in bed, whereupon he said that he had waited for us in order to announce to his mother and myself his engagement to Margaretta Nesmyth. The news evidently did not take his mother entirely by surprise; women are quicker than men in discerning affairs of the heart; but to me it was altogether unexpected. We congratulated him, of course, and wished him joy, and he went happily to bed to dream blissfully of his lady love.

" The first engagement in a family is an affair of decided importance, and for the rest of the night Leete's announcement quite drove from my mind all thoughts of the declaration of war. Upon questioning Edith I found that she had long had her suspicions that the two young folks were in love with one another, and that it would be merely a question of time before their engagement would be publicly announced. She spoke very highly of the young woman whose character she had evidently studied, and assured me that there was no doubt but that she would make our son an excellent wife. And then we fell to talking of our own courtship — a courtship that had more romance, in it than could be expected of any later lovemaking.

" This morning, however," Professor West continues, "the bulletin boards contained longer notices. A special session of Congress was called to meet in twenty days. All citizens were ordered to report at once to the Superintendents of their guilds the number of arms and amount of ammunition in their possession. The municipal authorities of the several sea-ports on the coast were authorized to take measures to protejet their harbors until such time as the authorities at Washington could formulate a plan of national defense. On the bulletins were also announcements that the heads of the local guilds would meet at noon to devise means of defense."

Constantly, in his diary, Professor West expresses his astonishment at the little excitement created by the declaration of war. To us in China, the calmness with which the United States received the news was unexpected and almost inexplicable. We knew of course that the whole tendency of Nationalism was to wipe out individualism and to train the individual to rely in all matters upon his rulers ; but we had not expected that this loss of individualism would be so complete as to prevent our declaration of war from being considered as a matter of personal moment to each individual. That such was the case,, however, is the unanimous testimony of all the survivors of the late invasion.

But while the people were in a state of blissful unconcern,

what were the rulers doing? We know, now, that they were in a state of great perplexity. As I have said before, they had been most unaccountably blind to the lessons which they should have learned from the events in France. Fatuously blind, they had taken no measures of national defense. They had lived and acted as if war was no longer a possible thing.[7] The government possessed not one single vessel of war, its marine was wholly mercantile or scientific. There was not one establishment among the thousands of manufactories in your country that could turn out a cannon ; there were only two that could turn out small firearms, and these were of trifling capacity, as the only demand for such weapons had been for sporting purposes. Your coast defenses had for a century been turned into public parks; your forts, into buildings for public recreation. There were few men among you who knew any thing of military science, and they had no practical training but had studied it only for amusement. You were absolutely defenseless, and it was no wonder that your rulers were perplexed.

As we look backward we may well ask, who was responsible for this state of affairs ? The responsibility rests on no one man or set of men. Your condition was the natural resultant of your form of government. Under the Nationalistic theory, a standing army in time of peace was a collection of idlers who added nothing to the resources of the State, but were none the less consumers. The same false process of reasoning forbade the existence of a navy. To have manufactured guns and to have stored up munitions of war would have seemed to the Nationalist theorist a waste of the resources of the nation. To have maintained military schools and to have required military service of each able-bodied citizen would have been to deplete the ranks of the workers. And when there came a time when you would have willingly mortgaged all your workshops and factories, all your material prosperity, thrice over, to have possessed the means of defense, you found too late that armies and navies do not spring up, full-armed and disciplined, at the biddings of Legislatures, and that munitions of war do not exist merely because they are wished for.

Had your ancestors heeded the lessons pf the French Revolution — had you learned your own weakness from the disasters that befell the Nationalist government of France — had you built ships capable of resisting any enemy and forts capable of defending your coasts; had you organized a standing army that might serve as a nucleus in time of war; had you required all citizens to know something, at least, of the profession of arms; had you even established military foundries and machine-shops — had you done all these, or only one of these things, it is probable that China would never have declared war with you; never have invaded your land; never have subjugated your ancestors; and, finally, never have imposed upon you the blessings of that civilization which has made the Celestial Kingdom ot China the greatest nation that the world has ever known.

You must remember that we in China were not ignorant of your defenseless condition. We knew all about it. Nationalism had subjugated all the nations of the world except the Flowery Kingdom. We recognized its merits, while at the same time we saw its defects. To us it seemed, at first, the attempt of barbarians to graft upon their social system a policy that had been in vogue in China for many years. Perhaps, had it been promulgated only by men of English descent, it would have retained the element of practicability — for the English, in all previous reforms, had been practical; but owing to the short-sightedness of your remote ancestors you had permitted your country to be over-run with emigrants from the slums of other nations; they had been given equal rights, socially and politically, and they had intermarried with your native stock until it became so debased that, one hundred years ago, your ancestors were as ready as the Frenchmen of the eighteenth century to abandon every thing for the sake of an idea.

At first, then, we in China thought that Nationalism was simply a barbarian attempt to imitate our own system of government. The grading system, which the Nationalists were so enthusiastic over, bore a remarkable likeness to our system of examinations ; and there were other points of resemblance which I have not, now, time to dwell upon. But, as the years passed, we became undeceived. We saw that you were trying a new experiment.

To prevent her people from being contaminated by the new theories, China enforced more strictly her policy of non-intercourse with other nations. We became more and more an isolated people. But the present century (I speak now by your ancient method of computing by the Christian calendar) had not commenced, before our statesmen saw that so passive a policy as non-intercourse would not suffice. An era of propagandism seemed to have set in, and emissaries from the outside world managed in various disguises to enter the Celestial Kingdom and to preach the pernicious doctrines of Nationalism.

It was then that our statesmen were convinced that sooner or later an appeal to arms would be necessary to preserve our own system of government, and it was then that China began to prepare for war. It was then that our Bureau of Foreign Intelligence was established, much on the same lines that it now follows; and then it was, that the system of compulsory mihtary service and training was required of every one of our citizens.

The Chinese have ever been a conservative nation ; and on this occasion, knowing the immensity of the stake they might have to play for— knowing that sooner or later the choice would lie between conquering the world or being conquered by it — we moved more slowly and cautiously than ever. In one generation China has been transformed into a vast camp where every able-bodied man is a soldier or a sailor, armed and equipped with the most recent weapons of war. Our surface and submarine navies are the finest that have ever yet been seen.

How much longer we might have continued our preparations there is no knowing. We saw the advantage which the growing discontent in France might afford an ambitious man — we found such a man in Ruy de Montalbon, chief of the guild of toy-makers in Marseilles; we furnished him with aid to scheme, and when the rebellion broke out at a preconcerted time we had munitions of war from our armories near at hand for his adherents.

It may with truth be said that it was China who changed the form of the French government and placed the present Emperor on the throne of France. And yet strange to say, not one nation of the civilized world took warning from the fact.

Professor West points out the reason of this fatal blindness, and later I shall dwell on it more at length. Suffice it now to say that the Nationalistic system when, under the mistaken idea that it was abolishing idlers, abolished the diplomatic corps, and allowed newspapers to decay, abolished really the eyes of the nation.

On the 29th of September, when we declared war against the United States, we had four fleets at sea. One was at Brest, and it was the duty of this to prevent Great Britain or Germany from sending you assistance. The precaution was wise though utterly unnecessary as the National system had rendered those two countries as helpless as the United States.

The second was more than half way across the North Atlantic.

The third was at anchor in the French West Indies.

The fourth was three days' sail from the Pacific coast of North America.

Each of these last three fleets was under sealed orders, which, being opened on the 29th of September informed it of the declaration of war and instructed it what to do.

Our North Atlantic fleeti was the strongest. It included six of our largest ironclads armed each with four pneumatic dynamite guns that had a range of fifteen miles; twelve light-armored cruisers each armed with one similar pneumatic gun and four guns of lighter calibre; two dispatch boats; and eight torpedo boats.

It was the duty of the light cruisers in this fleet to seize upon the swift ocean steamers plying between Europe and the United States, and convoy them to France, where they would be used as transports for the army which we had been accumulating there. The heavier war ships were to destroy any fortiflcations which might be erected on the coast, and to hold the principal cities to ransom until the arrival of the troops; the torpedo boats, two of which were submarine vessels, were to aid the war ships.

Fleet number three, composed of four of our heaviest war

vessels, with six attendant torpedo boats, was to take possession of the Gulf of'Mexico and the Mississippi, and to act in conjunction with the army when it arrived.

Fleet number four was composed of only two war ships, but these convoyed one hundred and two steamers on which was the army destined to begin the invasion of the Pacific coast.

Our plans had all been carefully prepared beforehand, and were executed without a miscarriage.

# Chapter 3 LECTURE III.

Let me now return to Professor Julian West's diary, continuing it from where we last left off, under date of September 30th.

" After breakfast," writes Professor West, " Edith informed me that she had put in a requisition for a young man and a young woman from our ward-house, and that she purposed, with their assistance, to devote the first half of the day to putting my study in order. This I took as a notice to absent myself until dinner time; and accordingly having seen that my more important papers were securely locked up, where they could not be disarranged, I wended my way to the college buildings. I found my lecture-room all newly-swept, and smelling somewhat of fresh paint and varnish, so after chatting a little while with such of the other professors as happened to be in the building, I went to the library and spent the rest of the morning there.

" We dined, as usual, at one, and I returned home in time to go with Edith and the children to our ward eating-house. After our meal was finished.

" Edith went back to her house-cleaning, while I went down town to the State House to learn what had been the outcome of the meeting of the heads of our local guilds. They had adjourned for dinner as I had expected, and were reassembling when I arrived. As I was personally acquainted with most of them, and as my position was to a great extent a public one, I was invited to remain and listen to the debates, and

I gladly accepted the invitation. We remained in consultation until darkness warned us that the supper hour was near, and then adjourned to meet again later in the evening.

" The measures agreed upon, were, practically, as follows : It had been agreed that ten per centum of the active force should be released from their occupations, and proceed, at once, to arm and drill and act as a local military force. This ten per centum was to be selected from the various trades by their respective Superintendents, who were given plenary powers of selection. They were to meet on the following morning and select the officers, who were to be subject to the commands of a Committee on Military Affairs, composed of members of the Municipal Council.

" Three of our most distinguished architects, and two civil engineers had gone down the bay to examine the coast defenses, and the guild yacht clubs had been ordered to hold their various boats in readiness for instant service. A committee of the Superintendents of the female guilds had been appointed to devise a uniform for the military, and was given authority to call upon the tailoring department for the necessary number of uniforms. Another committee, called the Committee on Munitions of War, was appointed and directed to procure at once as large an amount of powder and shot as possible, and was given authority to levy requisitions on the various machine-shops and chemical factories for these materials. The hours of labor were ordered to be lengthened in those trades from which the military were taken, so that there might be no decrease in the production corresponding to the decrease in the number of producers.

" The transaction of this business had consumed the hours of the day's session, and when the adjournment was ordered, I went home to supper.

"Arrived at home, I found awaiting me a message from the President of Shawmut College, which recited an order received from the Committee on Military Affairs and desired me to at once select ten per centum of the students in the Historical Section and to notify them to meet on the Common at nine o'clock the next morning to be mustered into the military service.

"A very hastily-swallowed supper sufficed me after I had read this communication, and then I hurried to the President's house, I was not his only visitor. The heads of every section of the college had received notices similar to mine, and, being perplexed as I was, had hurried to the President's house for consultation. Most of us were bothered in the same way; to each of us there was an incoming class of new students whom we had never met and whom we knew of only because their names were on the college lists; how could we intelligently select, as best fitted for soldiering, a percentage of a class which we had never seen. Besides there, was a point, which had not occurred to me, but which I found that a majority of my colleagues in the faculty were worrying over, and that was this: we were required to select ten per centum from our sections — did this mean that we were to select the ten per centum from the section as a whole, or a quarter of it from the senior, junior, sophomore and freshman classes, each, respectively? With these questions before us our chance meeting at the President's house resolved itself practically into an informal meeting of the faculty — some of my students were also in the classes of Professor Smith, Lecturer on Biology, and I was in doubt whether Prof. S. or myself should count such among our quotas.

"But when I got home, feeling quite satisfied that our deliberations had settled all matters so far as the college was concerned, I showed my list to Edith (who was sitting up for me) and was annoyed to find that she at once disapproved of it — because I had put down as the quota selected by me only men and had ignored the women who formed nearly half my classes."

I cease now for a time my quotations from Professor West's diary, because I can more succinctly narrate to you, in my own words what followed. I have quoted from his diary enough to show you how utterly unprepared for invasion your country was under the Nationalist system, and how entirely unsuspecting your governing people were of what was to follow. When Professor West wrote in his diary those entries which I have just read to you, the rulers of the United States were unanimously of the opinion that the first attack of China would be on the Pacific ports ; and no one had any idea that New England or the Middle or Southern States would ever be the scene of battle.

The preparations for simultaneons attack which we had made had passed utterly unnoticed by your rulers. This lamentable ignorance could never have existed if there had been a diplomatic corps abroad, or if there had been newspapers in any way resembling those published by your ancestors during the latter half of the nineteenth century. But such newspapers had been exterminated upon the universal adoption of the

Nationalist system. Government became the sole manufacturer and distributor of goods; advertising was at an end. As Professor West justly remarks in a letter dated A. D. 2001,[8] your general news you received officially, all alike, as it was given you ; and the official bulletins met all demands that arose, and gave all news which for public safety and morality it was deemed wise to publish. The theory of the Nationalist government, that a man who did not labor with his hands was an idler, prohibited the maintenance, in foreign countries, of a diplomatic corps or consular system which might have advised you, and surely would, of the contemplated attack of the Chinese; and as you had no navy and no standing army, you could have no military or naval agents abroad to report to their respective departments what other nations were preparing to do. Hence, as I say, you were in utter ignorance that great preparations had been made by China to attack some nation, and equally unaware that we contemplated a simultaneous invasion upon the east, west and south coasts of the United States.

I have been asked what the real cause of this war was. As I have already told you, it was in reality a defensive war undertaken by China to crush out the Nationalist theory of government. When a strong nation desires to go to war with a weak one, any pretext, no matter how trivial, serves as excuse for the declaration of hostilities. In this case I believe that the cause given was that a Chinese of high rank had been hooted in the streets of San Francisco, but the real reason was that China was so strong and you were so weak.

The United States rested in false security. Having become accustomed to believe war a thing of the past, you took no measures to preserve your powers of self-defense. You were soon, however, to be undeceived.

On the 1st day of October a fleet of vessels was spied off the coast of Maine. Spy-glasses were at once brought to bear on it, and as it approached, it was seen to consist of war vessels. The news was at once telegraphed to Boston and the other coast cities and to Washington.

The day had been cloudy, and night fell earlier than usual, but not before the strange vessels had approached near enough to show that they flew the national ensign of China. That night, for the first time, the Bostonians awoke to a realization of the threatened danger. Let me quote from some pencilled notes which I found among Professor West's papers. He says:

" We had been all sound asleep, when we were awakened by a tremendous knocking upon our front door. My wife heard it first, and aroused me, and I went to the window and looked out. It was a dark night, and at first I could see no one, but on calling out I was answered by a voice, which I recognized as belonging to one of the college janitors, and which said to me, as nearly as I can recollect the words, 'There's a Chinese fleet off the Cape, Professor, and the President wants you to meet him and the other professors at the State House right away.' To be startled from sleep by such a summons as this was not conducive to calm reflection. I dressed rapidly, and taking a hasty leave of Edith, hurried to the State House, where I found the Municipal Council and the larger part of the college faculty.

" The danger that confronted us was so sudden and unexpected that we could devise no way to meet it. There were indeed many plans proposed, but none, when examined, seemed to promise practical relief or protection. For the first time then I realized that we were practically unprotected. It was easy to call upon all citizens to arm, but they were undisciplined, and there were no weapons for them. It was easy to fasten cans of dynamite on the bows of every vessel in the harbor, but for such puerile attacks the invading forces would care nothing. And when we telegraphed to Washington for advice we were only told to do the best we could, and informed that similar fleets had been seen in the Gulf and at the entrance of Puget Sound.

" '*Do the best you can*,' that was all the help we got from the much-praised government at Washington."

There was a tendency in those days to hold the government, and by the government I mean the functionaries at Washington, responsible for the declaration of war and all the trouble that followed; but, as I have already suggested to you, it was your system of govern meut rather than your rulers that was responsible.

The fleet was seen off the coast on the afternoon of the 1st of October, at daybreak on the 2nd it was at the entrance to Boston Harbor and the city lay at the mercy of its guns. At nine o'clock a torpedo boat, flying a flag of truce from her bow, came steaming slowly up the channel, feeling her way cautiously as if fearful of torpedoes or submarine mines, for here let me observe that, although we in China were aware of your unprotected condition, we could not for one moment flatter ourselves that you were utterly unaware of our preparations for your invasion nor believe that the arrival of our fleets would find you so utterly unprepared for resistance.

Well, as I said, the torpedo boat came slowly up the

harbor. It was seen as it started and its approach was telephoned to the State House, so that a committee of the municipality met it at the wharf. It bore, as had been rightly conjectured, an officer from the fleet with a summons for the immediate surrender of the city and a demand for a ransom equal to about fifty millions of dollars. The refusal, of either of these demands, it was stated, would be followed by a bombardment of the city.

The sensation, which followed the arrival of this messenger, may be best described by an eye witness. I quote from an anonymous manuscript, now in the college library, the writer of which, though his name is not known, was one of those drafted from the unclassified grade of common laborers. He says:

" I was on the Common much earlier than was called for, but I was by no means alone. Men and women, who had been drafted from the other trades, were there also, and the air was fairly noisy with talk. The arrival of the fleet off the mouth of the harbor was known to most of us and was the principal topic of conversation, though there was also much discussion as to the uniforms we were to wear and many guesses hazarded whether the women, who had been selected, would be mustered in as a separate force or be apportioned with the men to different regiments.

" At nine o'clock, promptly, our Superintendents appeared upon the scene, and the quotas from the various guilds gathered around them and the lists of the selections were read, those present answering 'here,' and the few who were absent being marked accordingly. We had expected to be mustered into service immediately, but were told that the municipal authorities did not feel competent to decide the propriety of enrolling women, and had telegraphed to Washington for instructions on that point. We were told, therefore, to wait where we were until this point had bieen decided.

" About ten o'clock we received news of the torpedo boat's approach, and almost immediately afterward of the envoy's landing. Our Superintendents then appeared clearing a way for the committeemen and the envoy.

" The crowd by this time was very great. Every window in the neighborhood was packed thick with heads, but I was fortunately agile enough to climb a tree beneath which the envoy passed, and so I had a full view of him. He was a good-looking, well-made Chinaman of probably thirty-five years of age,[9] dressed in loose trousers of dark blue silk and a loose, flowing robe or shirt of yellow flowered damask, belted around his waist with a sword belt. He was accompanied by a guard of four fierce-looking sailor-men, armed to the teeth, but the things that struck us all as most curious were the long tails of hair that hung down their backs from underneath their helmets. They passed through the crowd into the State House, where the Municipal Council was assembled.

" In about an hour the envoy came out again, escorted as before, and disappeared in the direction of the wharf, whence in a little while we heard the sound of cheering — though what there was to cheer at none of us on the Common knew."

Now let me tell you what happened in the State House. His Excellency, Lieutenant Hi, delivered his demands, amid the most profound silence. He was empowered, he said, to allow one-half hour for deliberation, at the end of that time he should expect an answer. Having thus delivered himself he retired into one of the adjoining committee rooms. The perplexity of the Municipal Council was very great. Without special authorization from the central government it had no authority to grant the demands of the invaders, and a refusal to grant them meant the destruction of the city. To telegraph to Washington was a matter of course but no reply could be obtained from that city. This silence which added so much to the perplexities of the council we now know was owing to the confusion that reigned in Washington. Chinese war ships had appeared off the mouth of the Potomac, and the government archives were being hastily packed for removal and the officials were preparing for flight.

Telegrams from New York and Philadelphia showed a similar state of affairs. Boston could evidently expect no outside aid.

The half hour was extended by the Chinese envoy to an hour, but the more the council debated, the more inevitable and unavoidable seemed compliance with the Chinese demands. Every instinct prompted a refusal. To yield so readily was an offense to patriotism and self-respect — and yet to resist meant to resist hopelessly, meant the destruction of thousands of human lives and acres of art and architecture.

Reason pointed out clearly the folly of resistance; pride showed plainly the shame of yielding.

— —

Note.—The letter by Professor West referred to in the preceding lecture is as follows:

A Journalist's Confession,

Boston, A. D., 2001.


(Communicated through Dyer D. Lum.

Published by permission of the Open Court.)


You will be surprised, my dear Dr. Leete, to learn that I have severed my connection with the *Trumpet of Liberty*, but such is the fact. Your kindness in the past, your earnest zeal in laboring to secure sufficient subscribers to reimburse the executive power for expense incurred, as well as your unfailing optimism even when circumstances looked dark, all alike convince me that I would be derelict to favors received were I not to lay before you the reasons which have actuated me in this final step. Nor are the reasons purely sentimental, though I know that if I should place them upon that ground I could at once command the tender sympathies of your generous and trusting heart. And if my private criticisms herein as to the wisdom of our mode of conducting newspapers should seem to lean toward treason, I can but simply throw myself upon your good nature.

The imperative necessity of first securing enough subscribers to guarantee cost before permission to publish could be obtained, necessarily made the venture in a large degree local. To the circulars sent out, the replies from a distance were, as we expected, not very encouraging; the utter lack of advertising, if I may be permitted that antique word, prevented the fact from being widely known, as well as the character and scope of our work, and at the same time deprived us of means to collect names. In fact, my dear doctor, while in no wise depreciating the calm security we now possess of knowing that our material wants will be easily gratified, it still seems to me, but without indorsing Carlyle's allusion to "pig's wash," that this security of the stomach tends to confine our efforts within narrower circles and restrict our intellectual horizon within the boundaries of personal intercourse. Without means to reach unknown inquirers, our work and progress has been largely retarded.

But the *Trumpet*, fortunately, having a goodly subscription list, and I being elected editor, these difficulties were surmounted, even if it prevented a material reduction in terms or increase of attractions. But here a greater difficulty arose. You remember the biting sarcasms in works of a former age in which the clergy were assailed for being necessarily subservient to the pews whence arose their support. I fancy I can put myself in the place of a clergyman under those semi-barbarous conditions prevailing before government kindly relieved us of the care of overlooking our own morals. For even under our resplendent liberty, which I have done so much to trumpet, I have found myself continually treading on tender corns and drawing forth indignant protests from my constituency. Our beloved institutions have not fostered criticism; on the contrary, the tendency is plainly toward its repression. Though our presses continually issue books, they, like papers, find great difficulty in reaching beyond a merely local market, which while heightening cost necessarily limits-circulation. To write for the "pews" only, so to speak, restricts independence; while independence either curtails my list of readers or changes its personnel, in either case depriving the paper of an assured and solid bads.

To antagonize those within immediate reach, whom everything tends to render extremely conservative toward speculations relative to wider personal liberty, and without means to reach others at a distance to whom such thoughts might be welcome, is but one of the many difficulties I have encountered. Individual initiative having long since gone out of fashion, in the collapse of the ancient system of political economy, it becomes more and more difficult to assert it in the economy of intellect. I am aware that the field of journalism is regarded as exempted from the general rule of authoritative direction and, like the clergy, left to personal merit to win success; still the universal tendency of all our institutions to militant measures and direction largely- invalidates the theory. This tendency to centralization, which has become the crowning glory of our civilization, is strikingly manifest even in journalism, despite its theoretical exemption.

The subscribers being, so to speak, stockholders, and persons whose every-day occupations and mode of living tend to disparage individual initiative, the first effect of any thing blasphemous to the sacred shrine of the commonplace is the appointment of a committee, or board of directors, by the subscribers whose chief functions consist in promoting solidarity among the enrolled subscribers. Theoretically, I had become convinced that this was the flower of our civilization and frequently elucidated its philosophy at Shawmut College, but my later experience has not led me to be enraptured with its fragrance. Each one, in so far as individuality has survived, to however slight a degree, feels not only competent but authorized to express himself editorially; for those most fervent in presenting the superiority of collective wisdom are equally convinced that they are its organs.

When I accepted the position as editor I believed that this reservation of journalism from collective control was wise, but what was excluded in theory reappears in practice. If you could but look over the articles I have received from the stockholders whom I represent, the "pews" to whom I preach, you might be tempted to change the name of the paper to the *Scrap-Book*, or face the problem of reducing material cost without increasing intellectual costiveness. You see my dilemma; if I insert them I am publishing contradictory principles, if I exclude them I am flying in the face of our great and glorious institutions by looking backward to outgrown conditions, wherein some of your semi-barbarous forefathers were wont to prate of the inseparableness of personal initiative and responsibility.

That our social system can be criticised by writers for its compulsory enlistment for three years to secure ample supply for social demand for sewer-ditchers, night-scavengers, domestic service, etc., you would undoubtedly agree with me in regarding as only coming from those in whom our beneficent institutions had not eradicated as yet the hereditary taint of being " born tired," a complaint of which we read in some ancient authors. Yet, whatever its source, such criticisms are received, though generally concealed in allegory. Thus, recently, I had to reject a story of considerable literary excellence, wherein was described a fancied society where parity of conditions rendered free competition equitable, and remuneration for work was determined in open market by intensity and degree of repugnance overcome, thus unsocially offering the highest inducements to disagreeable labor. I saw at once the anarchistic character of the work, and promply suppressed it as treasonous.

I have also come to the conclusion, my dear Dr. Leete, that the newspaper is obsolete. For current gossip and small talk we already have abundant vehicles; for criticism on public polity there is no room, even if there were need, nor would it be wise to tolerate it in a community where individuality is subordinated to general welfare and protection constitutes the genius of all institutions. Our general news we receive officially, all alike, as it is given to us, and the official bulletins meet all demands that may arise which public safety and morality deem wisdom to publish. Titles of heavier treatises than the ephemeral requirements of newspapers may always be found in the official record of publications distributed among our purchasing agencies, to those who have time to search through their voluminous bulk, and even if a title should prove misleading, a common misforturne for which I can suggest no adequate remedy, our material prosperity is so well assured that credit so wasted will not injure any one.

Finding, therefore, that our present legally instituted scheme of journalism is incompatible with our social constitution, to preserve which all else must be sacrificed, in that it cannot be successfully conducted without individual initiative, control and responsibility, I gladly cease the struggle, to return to my chair of philosophy of history at Shawmut College. My own opinion is that the collective direction now so simplified over production and exchange in material fabrics, should be logically extended to the production and exchange of the more subtle fabrics of the brain if our glorious institutions are to permanently remain on a solid and immovable basis. To admit anarchy in thought, and insist on artificial regulation of relations which are born of thought, is plainly illogical and dangerous to collective liberty. A social system once instituted must be preserved at all hazards; to preserve is as essential as to create; and this is the more evident when we are the creators and know the result to be to our social well-being.

Happily, the compulsory solidarity to which civilization

has now attained in material wealth, and the moralization of militancy a century ago, effected by political high-priests, already gives every indication of being dominant in the intellectual sphere before the close of this newly-opened century. Having organized liberty, having brought the spirit of freedom down from abstract heights to add a local habitation to its name, by excluding individual initiative and personal responsibility in economics, having substituted the kind fraternalism of direction for the wild freedom of competition, let us hasten the rapidly-nearing day when intellect will also reject these survivals of a ruder age — a day wherein we will reach the culminating point of our civilization, where looking forward will be synonymous with looking backward!

Yours for organized and instituted liberty,

Julian West.

P. S. — Edith sends love; the baby is well.

J.W.

*Chapter 4 LECTURE IV.*

In considering the perplexities which beset the United States in these days we must remember that for over a century the Christian world had dreamed of war as a by-gone thing. As far back as 1890, one of your American thinkers, by name Frederick W. Ayer, prophesied,

" I am against war as an approved method of settling national disputes. Individuals are quarreling among themselves the world over; what would be our situation if these countless millions of disputes were to be settled in the arena by mutual blows instead of in the courts of law established for their arbitration? Boards of arbitration with high courts of appeal and last resort should be and will yet be, created for the hearing and adjustment of national and international complaints. Such courts already exist in fact, if not in form, by the mutual assent of nations. The rulers of the several countries of Europe are daily passing upon and settling by mutual consideration of the difficulties involved, questions which a century ago would have plunged the same countries into war.

" You may be sure that the trend and bent of modem diplomacy is against war. War possesses a terror for our civilization which it did not possess for the ages which have gone before us. Statesmanship no longer consists in fomenting quarrels between nations, and rulers must now answer to humanity instead of to kings. The heroes of the future will not be found on the fields of slaughter and the destruction of human life in settlement of national disputes will cease to be glory."

Such was the dream of your ancestors in 1890. The dream became a reality when the Nationalists succeeded in establishing your former government; but misled by their earnestness, blinded by their enthusiasm for ideas, they refused to see that as long as any one nation declined to submit to arbitration and persisted in maintaining a perfect apparatus of war, that one nation did of necessity because of its superior strength become the master of all those nations which disarmed. This folly was universal. No Nationalist teacher but was firmly convinced that war was a thing of the past, a barbarism of remote ages.

Imagine a community that has lived for a century upon the fertile slopes of a volcano, firm in the belief that the mountain was fast fixed and its fires long ago extinguished. Imagine the terror and perplexity of such a community, when suddenly they felt the earth beneath quiver and shake, while the sky became dark with smoke and ashes, and streams of fire flowed through their fertile vineyards and among their homes. Imagine such a community, and you can then gain some idea of the confusion that prevailed in the United States, when almost simultaneously there came the news that four hostile Chinese fleets held the great seaport cities of the nation at their mercy. It was a disaster too great for belief; men's minds could not grasp it.

The hour passed and his Excellency Lieutenant Hi appeared for the answer. There was no answer for him. The conflicting emotions in the minds of the Municipal Council had prevented reason from coming to a decision. Now, however, there could be no more delay. The Chinese envoy awaited an immediate reply.

A silence, as of the dead, reigned through the hall when

for the last time the envoy demanded an answer and refused further time. For a space there was a stillness so intense that men heard the palpitation of their hearts; and then the chairman of the meeting rose, and with a voice tremulous with emotion said : " Oh, my brothers ! What shall our answer be ?" And then, breaking the silence that for a little space ensued, the secretary's voice was heard calling the names of those who were to answer. " Charles Packer Bellamy " he said, and from the seats there arose a tall, spare form and answered:

" If to say 'No!' meant only death to me, then would I say 'No;' although a thousand deaths awaited me. But it means more. ' Twould doom to death others than myself — my wife, my little ones, my neighbors and my friends ! So, though my heart is ready to break with grief and shame, what can I do but answer 'Yes' ? "

And so, one after another, the members of the council answered "Yes;" and Boston was surrendered to a foreign foe.

We cannot doubt the unanimous testimony of those who being then present afterward recorded what their. saw. Never in the world's history had there been a scene like this. Strong men were sobbing like children. Eyes, that had been dry for years, dropped now the salt tears of anguish. That night there were many suicides.

I leave you to picture to yourselves the scene. In the years to come it will be the most dramatic scene in history, and will no doubt afford novelists and dramatists the base of many a plot.

But a little while ago, and I asked you to appreciate the perplexities of the Municipal Council by symbolizing them — you will remember my imagery of a people dwelling on the hillside of a volcano; now I ask you to picture to yourselves, a nation that for a century has built its hope and pride upon a theory, and finds, too late for any remedy, that though the theory is right, it has nevertheless destroyed itself by neglecting the simplest precautions of self-defense. And yet who can picture this ? I cannot. I doubt if you can. We can only stand afar off and wonder; yes, we can only wonder — that is all ! A navy, though weak, would have been a temporary defense. Forts and coast defenses, however antiquated, would have at least postponed for a little while the terrible humiliation of immediate surrender. A standing army would, by affording a nucleus for volunteers, have held the enemy in check until the raw troops had been levied and drafted, and the possession of factories capable of turning out munitions of war would have given hope of ultimate success to every individual act of resistance.

Yet not one of these were in existence — there were no forts, no navies, no standing army, no armories, no manufactories of arms. To have maintained such would have seemed to the rulers of that day the maintenance of an idle class — and an idle class was the one thing that the founders of the Nationalist system of government hated above all other things. They were terribly short-sighted. They realized that a man might work one hour a day and do nothing the other twenty-three hours, but they could not realize that a man might do nothing for twenty-three years and yet perform labor of inestimable value in the twenty-fourth. Because they were so short-sighted, life and treasure were wasted. Because their policy was the trivial one of immediate benefit you ultimately lost all they had been striving to gain. To be sure it is fortunate that this is the case; for otherwise you would never have known that higher civilization which my nation has given you.

That night, an hour before sunset, the fleet moved nearer to the city, and the next morning the citizens were awakened by the unaccustomed sound of sunrise guns. About eight o'clock a detachment of Chinese troops was landed and marched to the munlcipal buildings, and to the railroad, telegraph and telephone stations. Orders were promulgated requiring the citizens to proceed as usual to the workshops and forbidding any departure from the city without a pass from the Municipal Council. And that council sat all day in the State House practically prisoners of the invaders.

I have previously called your attention to the difficulties which beset the Municipal Council; I wish now to invite your consideration of the perplexity that embarrassed the commander of the Chinese fleet. His ships carried full complements of officers, marines and sailor-men, but these were counted by hundreds, while the Bostonese were counted by millions. To take the city into military occupation was, therefore, an impossibility, and his whole effort was to retain such control over it that the army then on its way from France might on its arrival be at once landed and distributed throughout the town. The city was, therefore, still governed through its former rulers, but these were in the charge of officers who understood English, and as I have already said, were practically prisoners. Their deliberations were also confined to the best method of raising the amount of ransom promised to prevent the destruction of the city; at least one Chinese officer, who understood English, being continually present to prevent any discussion as to ways or means of defense.

Here again appeared another weakness for which Nationalism was responsible. The Chinese naturally demanded that the ransom be paid in gold or silver money ; but of money there was none in the United States. There were no bankers nor banks ; no bills of exchange — no facilities for raising loans. True there was a large amount of the precious metals, in the shape of jewelry, plate and so forth, but this was the private property of the individuals, not of the municipality of Boston nor of the general government. There were jewels of great value known to be possessed by individual citizens, but under the Nationalist theory they were not the property of the State nor could they be used by the Municipal Council nor pledged by the authorities with the Chinese. So closely had the demand and supply, in all manufactured things, been regulated by the statisticians at Washington, that there was not even a surplusage of them to pledge. What had seemed to the Nationalist theorists the perfection of Nationalism, was now the ruin of the country. The United States was in the position of a man who having just enough money to pay for his dinner, is suddenly asked to pay a note for a large amount.

It had been surmised by the Chinese that the coast cities would be unable to pay the ransoms demanded; but it was recognized that such demands might serve to distract the public mind from the real purpose of the Chinese (which was the permanent occupation of the country); and that by protracting the negotiations as to the times, installments and manner of payment, a certain uncontested control of the city might be continued until the arrival of the army would permit a military occupancy. The delay also enabled the Chinese officers to study the city from a tactical standpoint, and to decide in exactly what places it would be best to place the army of occupation.

The Municipal Council was, therefore, encouraged to believe that some methed might be ultimately devised by which the ransom would be paid and accepted, and the city relieved of its foreign visitors. Nay, so far was this belief actually entertained by the Bostonians that there was actually some talk of giving a ball to the Chinese!

I could hardly believe this fact when it was first stated to me, but it was vouched for by so many authorities, that, ultimately, I could not but accept it as a truth. Yet, after all, it was but an illustration of the inability of a people to understand what they have been taught to believe was impossible to happen. It shows how thoroughly the Bostonians considered the visitation of the Chinese as a merely temporary incident. There was scarcely a person in Boston who did not think that the ransom would be paid, and the Chinese take their departure. To the Bostonians indulging in delusions of hope, the Chinese instead of enemies were simply visitors — unwelcome visitors, indeed, and visitors whom it was wise to propitiate, but still visitors.

Since I have come to realize that the intention to give a ball to the Chinese is an incontrovertible fact, I have often thought that it is an excellent example of that strange inability to realize the possibility of war, which sometimes permeates nations which have long been at peace.

*Chapter 5 LECTURE V.*

Let me quote again from Professor Julian West's diary. He narrates the events attendant upon the arrival of the fleet, the landing of the envoy, the deliberations of the council — which I have already sketched out to you — and then continues:

"It was six o'clock, supper-time. My heart was very heavy as I walked homeward, but Edith and the children were awaiting me, and all were so happy that I was loth to let my own grief intrude i upon them. And yet I could not wholly dissemble nor be quiet, and as we walked to the ward restaurant I mentioned some of my fears to Edith. She laughed them to scorn, and bade me not frighten the children. Later in the evening, when we were by ourselves, we had another talk, but still she would see nothing alarming in the situation. To her mind the invasion of the Chinese was but a temporary incident ; we would pay them so much of our goods, agree to pay them so much for several successive years — and they would then go away.

" The hours of labor might be lengthened a little, but that would be the only result. As for any danger coming near us or our family, she ridiculed the idea. Alas, I could not agree with her, though I knew, from what I had heard and seen, that her opinion was the opinion of our rulers and people. To me the vista of the future years seemed to open out into a long-continued war, and my youth was near enough to the great Civil War of 1861 to give me some idea of what the anguish and cost of war was.

" For many years I have been one with the people of to-day ; they have been my brothers and my sisters. Their ideas have been my ideas, their time has been my time, their era my era. But now I feel myself a stranger in a strange land. To those about me war is a word, and not an awful thing. Those to whom I have ventured to breathe my thoughts have looked upon me as weak, unmanly — almost as insane. To their minds there is to be no bloodshed — we will pay the Chinese and they will go away — they will arbitrate their grievances (but what those grievances are I have found no one who knows) — to take advantage of their strength and our unprepared condition would be too base for any nation to seriously contemplate — the dust of the old order of things was about me, blinding me, when I spoke of war and bloodshed, of rapine, battle and conquest — such are the answers I have received to-day when I have ventured to tell my thoughts.

" God grant that I be wrong and that all the others be right.

" I have endeavored to impress upon Edith the expediency of herself and the children leaving town. They could easily go back to the Adirondack cottage whence we have just come. But all my entreaties have been in vain. Edith insists that she cannot leave without the consent of the Superintendent of her guild, and that the children cannot go away unless their teachers have granted permission. I feel that I am powerless, and that I can do nothing but wait the events which to me are inevitable. I am alone in my ideas, not one, besides myself, of all the millions of Boston, thinks as I do."

Under the date of the next day, there is no entry in Professor West's diary, but under the date of two days later (October 4) he writes :

" The night before last I could not sleep for anxiety, and early in the morning I arose, and sought Dr. Stephen Bard, Edith's Superintendent, and procured from him a leave of absence. Then I procured similar leaves of absence from the children's teachers, though not without trouble. I spoke to Edith again, at breakfast, about going away, but found her very unwilling to leave town, and inclined after her night's rest to take even a more hopeful view of the situation than she had taken the night before. At half-past nine I went off to my lecture-room, with a heavy heart, passing on the way a body of Chinese marines who were about to take possession of the college telegraph and telephone office. It was the first symbol of foreign occupation, and oppressed me most distressingly.

"At dinner I was delighted to find that Edith had changed her mind, and was no longer opposed to leaving town. It appears, that moved by my entreaties of the morning she had gone to the railroad station to ask about trains, and had been informed by the Chinese officer in command, that she would not be suffered to depart, the officer adding what probably he intended as a compliment, but what Edith did not consider as such, that so pretty a woman as she could not be spared from the city. Whether it was this compliment that turned the scale in favor of departure, or the instinctive desire of her sex to do what is forbidden, I do not know. At all events she was now determined to leave town. But how ?   With the railroads guarded, and the surrounding waterways patrolled by the electric launches and torpedo boats of the Chinese, the two most natural avenues of escape were cut off. By order of our Chinese conquerors all the horses in the city had been surrendered to them, and were now corralled under a Chinese guard. For her and the children to walk was not for a moment to be considered.

" At last it occurred to us that we had at our own disposal an ancient animal that Dr. Leete had purchased a year before his death and which we had kept from motives of sentiment, and as this horse was of no use to any of us, he had been kept at pasture on a farm some five miles out of town. It was decided that this animal should now make some return to us. To bring him into the city while it was yet daylight might result in his confiscation ; it was, therefore, determined that Leete should at once go to the farm and see that the old creature was fed and ready for me when I should call for him about nine o'clock. We had in our stable a light sort of carryall, which we sometimes used in summer to drive about the country, and this was to be our ark of refuge.

" Having thus determined upon the means of flight, the next great question was as to what necessities and valuables might be taken. Clothes for Edith and the children were the first necessities, though I cautioned Edith to make these as few as possible, and to choose warm materials that would wear well, but in the end I had to discard fully one-half of what she selected, and what we took was packed in sacks and stowed under the seats for the sake of lightness.

" There was, however, a provision which I insisted upon, though Edith told me plainly that she thought me very foolish for so doing. Wheni I was discovered by Dr. Leete, I had in a safe within my chamber several thousand dollars in gold. This, being useless as money, had, with the exception of a few pieces given away as curiosities, remained intact; and this was what Edith, much against her will, took with her. Edith's jewels were also taken.

" During the afternoon I hurried to the college and obtained from the president leave to be away for a few following days, for I determined to accompany my family until I could feel assured that they were at least on the way to safety.

"Our preparations consumed the whole of the afternoon. At seven o'clock, after a hasty supper, I started to walk to the farm. It was a clear starlit evening, and a moon wpuld rise shortly after midnight, and I was glad to see as I walked along that the roads were in good condition. At half-past eight I reached the farm-house and I found old 'Galen' (for so Dr. Leete had named his steed), ready bridled for me. After a short rest I mounted him and rode homeward, leaving Leete at the farm which we would pass on our way out. I got home without incident about eleven, and we soon had 'Galen' harnessed to the wagon.

" We had promised ourselves that we would start at midnight, and as the hour of our leaving grew near, I noticed for the first time that Edith seemed to appreciate the sadness of our flight, the importance of the step we were taking. In this house we had lived since our marriage; here our children had been bom; here four of them had died. When the time came for us to leave it; we seemed to have a prescience that we should never return to it. A little before twelve, leaving the children in the wagon-house with the horse and the carriage, Edith and I went through the house once more. I saw the tears running down her face as I helped her to her seat in the carriage; and so, secretly and in sad silence, we left our home.

" Avoiding the thoroughfares, we drove through the less-frequented streets. Out on the country roads our hearts grew lighter; the children talked a little, then dropped off into uneasy slumbers. At the farm we stopped, watered old Galen, and gave him half an hour's rest.

" But here Leete begged me to let him return to town. Though I asked him why, I had no need to put the question to him. What lover would care to leave his mistress amid dangers that he himself was fleeing from ? And yet, though it grieved me deeply, I could not yield to his request. I represented to him that I might at any time be obliged to return. That his duty lay in caring for his mother. And I promised him that when we had seen her and the other children in a place of safety, I would assist his return, and if necessary aid him to forward Miss Nesmyth to his mother's care. With a heavy heart he acknowledged the justice of my reasoning, and we started once again.

" We had still some fifteen miles to go, for I wished to reach the railroad junction at Butler, where I thought it might be possible to procure railroad transportation. But Galen was old and unused to labor, and the wagon was heavy with our six children, besides my wife and myself and our baggage, and we went but slowly. Leete and I, and even Edith, walked the greater part of the way. The country was wonderfully beautiful and peaceful in the clear moonlight, but we were too weary and too sad to appreciate its beauties. We stopped frequently to rest our faithful beast. The morn was breaking as we came into Butler. Driving to a hotel, I soon had Edith and the children in bed, and having seen Galen unharnessed and duly stalled, and leaving Leete to sleep in the carriage and act as custodian of our goods, I snatched an hour's slumber for myself.

" Waking about eight I bathed at the hotel and went down to the railroad station. I found that trains were running to Boston, but that since noon of yesterday no trains had come from the city. This state of things resulted in accumulating in the Boston yards nearly all of the engines and much of the rolling-stock of the three roads that met here. I was told that until a train came from Boston there would be no chance of procuring transportation to the West. The railroad officials were evidently nonplussed by the unusual state of aflfairs, but went on blindly obeying the orders from the main office in Boston. While I was talking to the station master, who seemed a very intelligent fellow, a freight train profusely decorated with red flags went by, and I, asking what this unusual display of danger signals meant, was told that about sunset of the day before orders had come from Boston to forward as rapidly as possible all the powder, dynamite and provisions that could be collected.

" I saw at once the full meaning and import of this. The railroad officials in Boston had obeyed the instructions of the Municipal Council, to accumulate munitions of war in that city, and had given orders accordingly to the division over which they had control; and so 'hide bound' had their minds been made, by the routine of Nationalism, which, by relieving them of all responsibility except obedience to orders, had never educated them to consider that circumstances might arise when such orders should be no longer followed, nor to regard the results of their obedience as a matter in which they had any personal interest — so absolutely mechanical was their obedience that they were actually now going on obeying the orders of the Municipal Council, although such obedience was actually denuding the country of war material and accumulating it in the possession of the enemy ! In the days of my youth such blind obedience as this would have been impossible. There was not a man on the railroad that would not have refused to thus aid and abet the enemy. The proceeding was so utterly foolish that it was hard to conceive of it as the legitimate result of the destruction of individualism; it seemed more credible to believe it the work of our enemies themselves, who, I was aware, held the Boston offices under guard — and yet I knew the Boston railroad officials too well to believe that they would yield to force or threats or obey others than their immediate superiors in the Municipal Council.

" In my surprise and fear I temporarily forgot my anxiety for the safety of my own family, and hurried to the office of the superintendent of this division — but he was deaf to all my arguments and pleadings. Such gross disobedience to the explicit orders of his superiors would, he said, be little less than treason. His duty was to obey the orders; if those orders were wrong the responsibility rested upon the chiefs of the railroad division in

Boston. He even implied that I was subjecting myself to danger in recommending disobedience.

" Disheartened by my failure I endeavored to obtain from him some means of transportation westward, but he would only say to me that I must wait until a train came from the city.

" By this time it was nearly ten o'clock and I returned to the hotel and breakfasted with my family. Then leaving two of the younger boys to guard our carriage, and taking Leete with me, I went again to the railroad station. No train had left Boston; there was nothing to do but wait, so I sat down hopelessly on a bench and gave Leete permission to wander through the yard, warning him, however, not to be beyond easy call. He came back to me in about an hour. ' Father,' he said, ' I've been thinking. Why couldn't we get a hand-car and go on that — you and I could work it, and mother and the children by sitting close, could ride.'

" I looked up at my boy with surprise, for it had not occurred to me to ask him for suggestions. He stood before me, smiling and yet anxious, a tall, well-made fellow of nineteen.

" ' Would we not be in constant danger of collision with a train?' I asked.

" ' I think not,' he replied. ' I have been talking with one of the yard men, and he says that the road is double tracked, and that all the trains coming this way will keep on the right-hand track, so that our only danger will be being run into from behind, and we can stop at every station and find out if any train has left here or Boston.'

" I rose from my seat and went with him to the station master and talked with that functionary about Leete's plan. He said he saw no danger in it. No train would use the up track until the Boston train came along, and we could very easily be informed of that at any station we might come to. Questioned as to our probable ability to work the car, he laughingly answered that we could probably work it for a litUe way. But the car was not his to dispose of; for permission to use it I would have to apply to the superintendent. So to the superintendent's office we went; there to be disappointed by the statement that a permit allowing us to travel over the road in a hand-car (a most unusual proceeding) conld only be granted by some high officer in Boston — and I knew that telegraphing to Boston for this permission, as the superintendent suggested, meant only tele-graphrag to our Chinese invaders.

" I was on the point of departing when Leete whispered to me and I turned back. That boy of mine proves himself to be — as we would have said in the days of my youth — a veritable Yankee — so fertile is he in resources. Taking me aside, he whispered that he had learned that there was a second-hand hand-car that had been advertised for sale, and that we might buy this. I returned at once to the superintendent and expressed my desire to purchase the hand-car advertised. He looked at me curiously, but answered, politely enough, that the sale of worn-out material was something that another department attended to, and touching a bell summoned a messenger who conducted us to the person who had charge of the sales of the undesired property of the railroads. On our way thither a happy thought occurred to me (and here let me set it down, though it has nought to do with what I would record as the history of the day — here let me say that during all these hours of anxiety, I have instinctively turned to the remembrance of those earlier days of my life, when it was every one for himself, and when men, knowing this, looked for safety to their own ability, and never thought of casting responsibility for personal success or safety on a paternal government (democratic or republican), and that there have occurred to me phrases, like that which I have just characterized in a 'happy thought,' which by some strange freak of memory, bring back images of ancient days — for as I wrote the phrase there rose unbidden to my mind a picture of the time when Edith Bartlett and myself laughed over an early copy of Burnand's clever book called 'Happy Thoughts' — well as I wrote, a happy thought occurred to me, and in pursuance of it I whispered to Leete, that from this on he must lead and I would follow, in other words, that he must buy the car and make it useful to us, and I would pay the piper. So when we came to the sales-agent of the road, Leete did the talking and I stood by a listener. The hand-car was valued at $100, but Leete jewed the price down to $75, at which he bought it, and producing his credit card had that amount punched from it. This sales-agent then desired to know where the, car should be delivered and Leete promptly answered at Jacksons (a station six miles up the road). Upon the agent saying that he would send the car up by the first freight train, Leete demurred and an argument ensued between them which ended by the agent agreeing to send the car that afternoon, with a couple of men, over the rails, to Jacksons.

A bill of sale was made out and carefully placed by Leete in his pocket, and then armed with an order for the forwarding and delivery of the car we wended our way back to the railroad yard. The yardmaster was speedily found and on presentation of our order showed us the car (which we found to be in fairly good condition) and designated two men to work it up to Jacksons. Arranging that it should be there by seven o'clock that evening Leete and I hurried back to the hotel for dinner, for it was now two o'clock; Leete explaining to me on the way that he had asked for the delivery at Jacksons because he thought we would attract too much attention if we started from Butler. He also told me that the railroad crossed the highway about a quarter of a mile above Jacksons and suggested that I might drive to this point in the carryall and that we might embark there. To further this plan, he proposed to go himself on the hand-car from Butler to Jacksons and thence to the crossing. I assented to this proposition and promised to start with the rest of the family about four and wait for him at the crossing indicated.

" Great news awaited us at the dinner table — for Edith had been industriously gossipping while we were away. There was a great riot in New York and that city had been bombarded by Chinese war vessels as a punishment for its refusal to surrender. Washington was in the hands of the enemy and the central government was en route, by special trains, to Chicago. A Chinese fleet had entered the Mississippi, and New Orleans was preparing to surrender. A Chinese army had landed at Seattle, in Puget Sound, and Chinese war-ships were steaming up the Oregon to Portland. From Boston there was no authentic news, only the vaguest rumors, but these all agreed that a vast number of steamers had arrived bearing thousands of soldiers and that the city was under martial law.

" All that I heard made me yet more anxious to get further inland and so after dinner, having impressed upon Leete the importance of losing no time, I had Galen harnessed and we started for the meeting place.

" The afternoon was oppressively warm and Galen appeared very tired and was exceeding sluggish so that it was about six o'clock when we crossed the railroad track above Jacksons. Leete was waiting for us and I found, much to my delight, that he had persuaded one of the railroad men to accompany us — at least during the night. He had also learned at Jacksons that no train had yet started from Boston, and he had procured some narrow boards and built a sort of picket fence around three sides of the car, ' so that,' as he expressed it, ' none of the children might fall off.'

" We unloaded ourselves and our goods on to the car, backed the empty wagon to one side of the road and unharnessing Galen, turned him adrift to get his living as best he might. 'Twas ungrateful, perhaps, to leave him thus to shift for himself, but we could not take him with us, nor could we spare the time to secure him quarters at any neighboring farm. The car was small for so many of us and it required some management to stow ourselves and our belongings upon it. I bade the children sit down along the sides, their feet hanging down astraddle of the pickets which Leete had nailed to the framework of the car. Their mother and myself took similar safe but undignified positions. Our baggage was piled behind us as much as possible out of the way of the workers at the levers, and so we started in the dusk of the evening, Leete and the railroad man furnishing the propelling power.

" About ten we made the station at Agamuck, had accomplished twelve miles more of our journey, and here we rested for an hour, replenishing our lunch baskets at the hotel and procuring especially a supply of drinking water, a precaution, the neglect of which had caused us some inconvenience for the past two hours. We also took pains to learn if any train had left Boston and found that none had.

" About eleven we left Agamuck and when a mile or so beyond the town Edith insisted that she and I should relieve Leete and the railroad man at the levers. I remonstrated at once against her taking part in so arduous an exercise, but she laughed at me and declared that she had many a time done harder work than this in the gymnasium. And so my remonstrance resulted, as many a remonstrance had resulted before, in her having her own way.

" Leete and the railroad man relinquished the levers to us and took our places; and though they had protested that they were not fatigued, they proved that their protestations were prompted by kindness rather than by fact, by almost immediately falling asleep.

" For the next two hours Edith and I toiled at the levers. At intervals of half an hour we stopped and rested for ten minutes; then resumed our labors. The night was clear and moderately cool. There was a faint breeze blowing, and every now and then a scent of apples in the orchards, or of the drying grass in some meadow lately mowed, made our way sweet with pleasant odors. The stars seemed to look down upon us kindly, and I thought of another flight more than two thousand years ago, when another father and mother fled under their dim light to save their offspring.

" The heavy freight trains appeared ahead of us, then rattled noisily past and disappeared in the distance. The clank of the levers and the grinding of the wheels made a monotonous music as we flew onward, sometimes passing over high fills where the country lay in sleep far beneath us, and sometimes winding through a rocky cut where a thousand echoes disturbed the stillness of the night. The moon rose as we labored on, and we flew from moonlight into shadow, and again from shade to light. The labor was hard for me, I knew it must be doubly so for Edith, but she would not admit that it was, nor did she complain.

" About three o'clock we came to a small way-station, and I confessed to Edith that I was worn out, and she admitted that it might be well to rest. So I opened the switch and we ran the car upon the siding, and then, leaning against our pile of luggage, holding each other's hands, we fell asleep.

" Sunrise awakened us, stiff and sore from the unwonted labors of the preceding night. There was a pond close by the station and there I and my sons recuperated our energies by a morning bath, and when we were dressed, Edith and her daughters followed our example. Breakfast was then in order, and we opened our lunch baskets and grew quite jolly over our *al fresco* meal. Then we embarked again and sped onward until eight o'clock came and we were in Putnam. Leaving Leete and the railroad man to finish their slumbers on the car, I took Edith and the children to the hotel while I started on a hunt to learn the news and find steam transportation further westward.

" The college had a training school at Pomfret, a town three miles distant, and at one time or another I had personally met most of the teachers. Thither, then, I went. There was no official news from Boston, for that city seemed to be cut off from all communication with the outside world, but there were private advices from Butler which told us what was happening or had happened."

## Chapter 6 LECTURE VI.

Here, for a while, I cease to quote from Professor West's diary. The news which he sets out therein is for the most part correct, so far as it goes, but it is meagre. Of the important events that were almost hourly taking place, we know now far more than he knew then. His diary is of inestimable value as contemporaneous history, and of no small value as literature, for what could be more pathetic than the scene he so hastily yet vividly outlines of parents laboring at unaccustomed toil, and through the silent hours of the night, to bear their slumbering children into safety; and what could be a more philosophic comment on the workings of the Nationalistic system than the action of the division superintendents of the railroads in shipping munitions of war to a city in the hands of a foreign foe. That it has fallen upon me to present his narrative to the world is something that I am deeply grateful for.

Great events were happening while the Wests were toilsomely fleeing westward. The North Atlantic fleet had divided off Cape Cod. Part of it went to Boston, as has been already told you, part to New York, part to Washington and part to Philadelphia.

New York, refusing to surrender, had been promptly reduced to ruins by the shells from the fleet and Brooklyn and Jersey City had suffered incalculable damage. The loss of life in this bombardment was something frightful. In the three divisions of the city over four millions of people were wiped out of existence or driven from their homes. The horror of the catastrophe appalled the world, but at the same time it evidenced to all the Nationalistic governments, as nothing else could have done, the irresistible power of the Chinese Empire and the folly of those nations which had dreamed of war as a thing of the past.

Washington had fallen without the firing of a shot, the President and the Generals of the grand divisions of the great departments or groups of allied trades, and the chief clerks fleeing westward on special trains with such of the national archives as they could carry in their haste.

Philadelphia was still deliberating with characteristic slowness, over her inevitable surrender; and New Orleans and the mouth of the Mississippi were dominated by the Chinese fleet in the Gulf.

The Pacific coast fared no better than the East. San Francisco, Seattle and Portland were in possession of Chinese armies, and every available vessel on the two oceans was engaged in swelling the numbers of the invaders.

At the beginning of the twentieth century (I speak according to the ancient Christian chronology) the population of China was nearly five times that of the United States. In the latter country, however, during the following century, the population had enormously increased. The fact that the nation guaranteed to each child that was born the means of subsistence had taken away one of the greatest checks of over population and as a consequence parents had given their sexual passions full sway and it was not an unusual thing for mothers to bear children every year. At the beginning of the twentieth century the average number in each family was five, at the beginning of the twenty-first it had risen to sixteen. The populations of the United States and of China had, therefore, become more nearly equalized.

The problem which confronted the statesmen of China

was nothing less than the implanting of the Chinese system of government on a nation of over two hundred million souls. This was considered an impossibility so long as the United States was inhabited by its native citizens, and, therefore, the Chinese, as soon as the army in this country was large enough to completely garrison the captured cities, began to remove the natives and replace them with subjects of the Celestial Kingdom.

On the afternoon of October 4, there arrived in Boston ships bearing five thousand Chinese soldiers. These were at once landed and stationed as a cordon around the city. Three days were given the vessels to unload and refit, and then five thousand of the flower of the young men of Boston were drafted for exportation. The consternation which this created may be more easily imagined than described; there was weeping and wailing in, those families which had sons between the ages of eighteen and thirty-five, and there was a rebellion among those selected for transportation, until the Chinese troops were called out, and one hundred thousand citizens were slain. There was a general attempt to leave the city, but those who succeeded in making their escape were comparatively few.

These methods were pursued in every city which was captured by the Chinese as soon as the army arrived in sufficient numbers to coerce the inhabitants. The swift Atlantic passenger and freight steamers were continually plying to and fro between France and America, bearing hither Chinese and French soldiers and artisans, and carrying to France an equal number of the flower of American young men. "Within six months after the declaration of war the whole eastern coast of the United States, for an average of one hundred miles inland had more Chinese subjects than native born Americans; while in the Pacific States, owing to their greater nearness to China, there were thrice as many Chinese as Americans.

The factories, workshops and farms were at once placed under the supervision of Chinese. Provinces were erected, their boundaries following as near as possible the old lines of the States, and a Chinese mandarin of the first rank placed as Governor over each. Thus in six months all the seaboard States had become dependencies of China, were practically part of the Chinese Empire, and the Nationalists were hemmed in on three sides — from the East, the South and the West.

The condition of those who were exported was indeed pitiable in the extreme. On board ship their feet were manacled to lessen the danger of insurrection. The vessels that carried them were necessarily overcrowded. The confined quarters, the vitiated air, the unavoidable discomforts of an ocean passage, and the dejection of mind of the unfortunates, all combined to generate diseases which decimated their numbers. And when they disbarked in France or China their condition was not much improved. Strangers in a strange land, not knowing the tongue of their masters, sold at private sale and public auction as laborers to whosoever would hire them, they became practically slaves. The mortality among them is frightful to contemplate, but we may well doubt if those who died were not more fortunate than those whose existence continued for a longer term of years. This wholesale deportation was then, and is now, considered excusable only as a frightful necessity of war.

Having thus rapidly sketched to you the events which were transpiring while the Wests were seeking an inland refuge, let me resume my quotations from my predecessor's diary and give you a contemporaneous narrative rather than my own analysis. After recording the news that he heard, Professor West says:

" It was, in a certain sense, gratifying to get news from Boston, even though it was bad news; and it was certainly a gratification to know that we had at least not actually been in error in fleeing from that city while there was yet time and opportunity to leave it. But our congratulations on our foresight soon gave way to anxieties to proceed further inland.

"I was utterly fatigued with the labors and anxieties of the past few days and I determined to sleep while Leete, who seemed as fresh as ever, went forth to learn if we could get an easier transportation westward than that which hitherto had been our fortune. As soon as he had left us I undressed, bathed and went to bed, recommending Edith and the younger children to do likewise.

" A few minutes afterward (as it seemed to me— though my watch showed that it was a full two hours) I was awakened by Leete who informed me that the regular local freight train was to leave for Worcester in thirty minutes and that he had secured a platform car for our hand-car and a box-car for ourselves. This, he said, was the best we could do, and he had not hesitated to engage the accommodation. I dressed quickly and we hurried to the depot. The train was almost ready to start, and amid the sly laughter of the bystanders, we entered the box-car—all of us excepting Leete, who preferred to ride with the hand-car. I think that nothing saved us from an open and probably offensive guying but the general knowledge that I was a professor of Shawraut College, and might, therefore, have some motive not comprehended by the crowd. However, the remarks that were made, and the inquisitiveness of the people, were so offensive to Edith that I closed the doors of the car, and we rode in darkness until several miles out of town.

" When we were fairly out in the country, and this stage of our journey had been safely commenced, I at once prepared for slumber, advising my children to do likewise, as there was no knowing when we might again have a chance for repose. The floor of the car was too hard for our slumbers to be soft, but at the second station from Putnam we stopped for quite awhile, and I bought a lot of hay which, being arranged at one end of the car, made fragrant and pleasant couches for us. We were all greatly refreshed when, at ten o'clock, we drew into Worcester. Edith and I and the elder children knew the town well, having often visited there, and their first thought was to make our arrival known to our friends; but for myself I had but one desire, and that was to hasten westward. Moreover, my leave of absence was only for a few days, and though this was an indefinite term, which might be made to stretch as long as necessary, I was desirous of placing Edith and the children in a place of safety as soon as possible, and of then returning to my post at Boston. For these reasons, as soon as we had left the freight car, I began inquiries as to transportation further on. There was a local freight leaving for Springfield at midnight, and I managed to have our two cars hitched on to this. The night passed quietly and uneventfully. For two or three hours before daylight a chilly rain fell, but we were under shelter, and our beds of hay were as warm as they were soft. Springfield was reached about breakfast-time, and we enjoyed a good meal at the station, and had our lunch-baskets thoroughly replenished. "

*Chapter 7 LECTURE VII.*

The diary of Professor West is so enticing that I have yielded to the temptation of quoting very largely from it. But it is time now to turn from it to a consideration of what was happening at other points. For though in my future lectures, delivered to the Junior and Senior Classes, I shall take up the important battles one by one, and go into their details, I shall endeavor, in the introductory discourses, which I deliver to you now, to give you a general history of events, not so extended as to bewilder with a multiplicity of details, yet not so concise as to preclude all color. The general model which I have endeavored to make my guide has been that excellent book by Rossiter Johnson which has proved its superiority to all other histories of the Civil War of 1861, by remaining, until the present day, a textbook in the schools.

Leaving the Wests, then, well on their way to a refuge, let us see what events were happening in New York.

I have already told you that while Boston had surrendered upon demand, New York had refused the demands of the Chinese envoy. This necessitated the forcible reduction of that city, a proceeding which was more wasteful of time than it was difficult. On receipt of the first news of the arrival of the Chinese fleet off the coast all the vessels in the harbor had been seized by the Municipal Council and sunk at the Narrows, completely blocking the entrance to the upper bay for all except small boats. The few antiquated cannon in Fort Hamilton Park and Fort Wadsworth Park were cleaned and loaded, and great things were expected from them; so far as looks went they were very threatening, and so far as noise was concerned they were very impressive, but the supply of powder and shot for them was very scanty and the armored ships of the invaders cared no more for them than for so many toy popguns.

As soon as the envoy had returned to his ship the bombardment was at once commenced. The watchers on the bluffs of Staten Island saw a line of blackness speed noiselessly from the turret of one of the Chinese ships, traverse for a moment an arc through the air, and then fall out of sight among the buildings of Brooklyn. There was a pause of a second or two and then a thick grey cloud of dust arose, widening and spreading as it grew higher, and from the distance came a dull report showing that the shell had exploded. Ten minutes later and a second shell fell in New York among the beautiful residences of lower Broadway, and after another ten minutes Jersey City was likewise visited by a messenger of destruction.

As if satisfied with these evidences of destruction, the Chinese now ceased their fire. We who live today know the reason. There was no wish on the part of the invaders to destroy property which they knew was sooner or later to be their own. They foresaw clearly that whatever damage was inflicted upon the cities must sooner or later be repaired by themselves — and they had no desire to lay out additional labor for their countrymen. The three shells, one to each of the three divisions of the city, were intended to convince the Municipal Council of the futility of resistance and perhaps also of the moderation of their invaders.

Unfortunately this moderation was wholly misunderstood. The mass of the people, owing to the short-sightedness of the Nationalistic policy, had never seen a war-ship, and the most ridiculous rumors prevailed about those which were now in the lower bay. It was commonly believed that these ships could only fire three shots a day, and there were not wanting engineers to show by figures that each discharge was, owing to the strain upon the ship, almost as disastrous to the invaders as to the invaded. Moderation was mistaken for weakness (as it so often is by men of little experience) and the spirit of the municipal councillors rose when it should have fallen.

Had there been then in existence a national standing army or a navy, it would have been impossible for the citizens to have so misinterpreted the generous moderation of the enemy.

It was now evening and as darkness settled down over the waters the bright search lights of the ships shone out, their torpedo nettings were let down and the sentinel steam-launches began their patrols. News of these strange evolutions was telephoned to the city and the night trains to the ocean beaches were crowded with people curious to see the sight. The most of the citizens were like curious children crowding to see a show. If it were dangerons, it was the duty of their nurses and guardians — that is their Superintendents and masters in the Municipal Council — to guard them from danger. Born to expect guardianship and support, without either being the result of personal forethought or experience, they could not now, suddenly, appreciate the need of individual reliance upon themselves. In fact, in their conduct, they illustrated the great weakness that Nationalism had wrought npon the character of the individuals who were subjected to it. Under Nationalism men had become mere routinists — theorists following a beaten track and blind to all things outside of it. Individual responsibility had received its death stroke when the rewards of individual initative and execution had become equalized.

There never was a truer proverb than that which tells us that "necessity is the mother of invention." In a new country, where the comforts and conveniences of civilization are few, and settlers are far apart from each other, each family has to rely upon itself, and the man who is most fertile in resources wins the prize of the greater comfort. But under the Nationalistic system, where all human beings were entitled, to an equal support simply because they were human beings, and where human beings were propagated *ad libitum*, there never before had arisen a necessity to quicken the ingenuity and self-reliance of the individual. As children, in the olden time, used to expect as a matter of course that their parents would protect and shelter, feed, and clothe them, so, now, the people of the United States expected that their rulers would guard them. The same exaggerated idea which the child has of his parents' powers and ability, the people of the United States now had in the ability of their rulers.

The morning of October 4th dawned without a cloud in the sky. Scarcely had the sun risen above the horizon when a steam launch was seen putting-off from the flag-ship and taking its way to New York. A flag of truce floated from its bow and evidently it bore some messenger from the invaders to the Municipal Council. It came up slowly, feeling its way — for it was fearful of torpedoes or submarine mines — and between the two fort-parks it stopped and signalled. These signals meant that it was a flag of truce and wished a pilot to the city. They could have been easily understood six score years before, but now there was no one high in authority who answered them. After waiting half an hour without a reply to its signals the boat proceeded cautiously on her way, passed safely over and through the obstructions in the Narrows and finally reached a landing in New York. It was now near nine o'clock and the three parts of the metropolis were alive to the boat's approach — for the telephone had announced its coming long before it appeared in sight.

The Municipal Council met the envoy as he landed and received his message on the dock. It was a merciful message, being merely a repetition of the summons of the day before — and yet he met only with defiance. It was in vain that he expostulated and represented the terrible loss of life that would result. His arguments were unavailing. With what is now inconceivable folly, the Chinese were bidden to do their worst; and the Chinese envoy was permitted to depart with a most bombastic answer to his summons.

To explain this foolishness of the Municipal Council of New York we must for a moment turn our attention to the history of the days preceding the establishment of the Nationalistic government. In 1861 there broke out a rebellion by certain States which set up an independent form of govemment. This rebellion had been planned long before it had broken out, and most of the munitions of war in the land had been transferred to those States which were about to rebel. Yet in spite of this, the inventive genius of the loyal States created and equipped an army and navy that astonished the world and revolutionized the pre-existing methods of warfare. After this war was ended and the army and navy were reduced to a peace footing, the idea prevailed very generally throughout the nation that in the event of another war the ingenuity of the American people would suffice to defend the nation when attacked. And when, upon the formation of the Nationalistic government, the army and navy were declared idlers that added nothing to the productive power of the nation, and were abolished, this same foolish idea about the ingenuity of the American people was generally accepted in excuse. Apart from the fact that Nationalism had dulled the inventive faculties by no longer making existence dependent on them, the most ingenious person can do little if he has no tools to work with, and no knowledge of things to be invented — and that was just the condition of the United States. The improved guns of the Chinese were the evolution of centuries of invention — but the ingenious American was expected to improve on these guns, which he had never seen and was totally unfamiliar with.

The Chinese envoy having returned, the ships opened fire, this time upon the fort-parks, which were speedily demolished. A few well-directed shells and automatic torpedoes scattered the obstructions in the Narrows, and at sunset of the 4th, the fleet was in the upper bay. For an hour, shot after shot fell in the three sections of the city. The bombardment ceased when the night fell.

But when the sun rose the next morning it looked down not only on the fleet of Chinese war vessels, but also upon two score transports that arrived in the early dawn.

For the third time an envoy came, under flag of truce, to the city, but there were no longer any in authority who met him. Some of the Municipal Council had been slain by the exploding shells, those who had escaped with their lives were fleeing up the Hudson. Finding that the city was governless, the envoy quickly returned and the troops were landed. The people of the city were like children in a school whose father has gone away. Without leaders they were powerless.

And then followed one of the most regrettable occurrences of the war—an occurrence justifled only by the necessity of making an example of the one city that as yet had had the temerity to resist the invaders. New York was given over to all the horrors of sack and pillage. Men, women and children became the property of their captors, goods and valuables of all kinds became the booty of the Chinese sailors and soldiers. Then followed rioting, when men rendered desperate by the cruelty inflicted on daughters, wives or mothers, rose in futile wrath and were shot down like dogs. It has been estimated that about two million people were killed in the bombardment, but the loss among the citiizeng during the rioting rose to almost one million.

As soon as order was restored, which was not until the 8th of the month, all the able-bodied men were chained together in gangs of one hundred, and made to clear the streets of the debris that had blocked them in consequence of the bombardment. On the 9th, fifty thousand of these workers, being the best of them between the ages of sixteen and forty were marched in their chains on board the transports which then left with them for France.

Since the 4th of October, there had been a constant exodus from the city, the inhabitants fleeing on foot, by rail, and in all sorts of boats or vessels. A very large proportion of them had fled up the Hudson, and urged by a common impulse had stayed their flight at West Point. At this place, endeared to Americans by its natural beauties as well as by the historic memories that surrounded it, the fleeing New Yorkers determined to make a stand for defense. A great quantity of dynamite was collected, placed in various receptacles and sunk as torpedoes in the river at this point. Crude slings, much like the catapults used by the ancient Romans, were erected along the shores to throw other masses of dynamite upon all hostile vessels that might come within range. Certain yachts had come hither with the officers of the yacht clubs that owned them, and these vessels were fitted out with long poles projecting from their bows at the further end of which was dynamite, gun-cotton, or some other explosive. With such crude means of defense the refugees at West Point awaited an attack.

*Chapter 8 LECTURE VIII.*

The 8th of October has come down to us in history, famous as the date of two historical events, the massacre in Boston, and the battle of West Point. Let us consider the massacre first.

I have already pointed out to you that one of the methods by which the Chinese expected to complete and perpetuate the subversion of Nationalistic ideas and the subjugation of North America, was by distributing native Americans through France and China, and bringing native Chinese to America. In pursuance of this plan, between five and six thousand young men were drafted from the trades in Boston, and on the morning of the 8th of October were collected on the Common. Only the highest Chinese officers were aware of the purpose for which they were collected. No suspicion of it had entered the minds either of those drafted or the populace of the city. Indeed, the full meaning of the Chinese invasion had not occurred to any number of the Americans, rulers or ruled. The popular, indeed, I might almost say, the universal and unanimous opinion, was that upon receiving payment of a ransom, the invaders would sail away, and that affairs would then go on as they did before — and all things be as they were, except that the nation might not be quite so rich as it had been.

When a notion is entertained by a people generally, it takes time to make many individuals among that people aware that the notion is erroneous. We must remember these facts when considering the ease with which the Chinese took possession of most of the great central cities of the United States.

No idea that they were to be deported had entered the

heads of the drafted men on the Common when they were formed in lines and the roll of their names was called ; but when the armorers of the war vessels appeared and carts containing chains and shackles were driven up, something of the truth became apparent. The lines wavered, then broke into disorder, and the attempt of the armorers to mancle those nearest to them, resulted in a rush that drove them back. Some such resistance was expected by the Chinese commanders, and the Common had been surrounded by a strong cordon of troops. These now advanced with fixed bayonets until the rioters were huddled in a disorganized, indignant, and terrified mass at one end of the Common. The bolder spirits among the Americans wrenched off the branches of the trees, and using them as clubs endeavored by a sudden rush to break through the ranks of the military. It was at this point that the word "fire" was given, and a murderous discharge was poured into the mass of unarmed, helpless rioters. Three volleys were fired with terrible execution — out of the five thousand Americans less than one hundred escaped unwounded, and these were promptly overcome by numbers, manacled and marched to the water-front. Permission was then given to the citizens in general to remove the dead and succor the wounded, and the Chinese troops in small detachments at once visited the different work-shops, seized on small percentages of the men they found there and placed them on board the transports, where they were chained together as they arrived. The. city was then divided into sections and each house was visited. All jewels, articles of gold or silver, and generally all the lighter and more portable valuables that could be found, were seized and carried away. The city was declared to be under martial law, and the inhabitants threatened with death if found out of doors after dusk.

While these events were happening in Boston, part of the Chinese fleet off New York had sailed up the Hudson with the intention of receiving the submission of the smaller river cities, and of establishing a depot for further operations at Albany. This naval detachment consisted of two armored cruisers, two torpedo boats, and ten steam launches.

It proceeded as far as Peekskill without incident, the municipal authorities in every instance, rendering submission without, in most cases, even a show of resistance. At Peekskill the Chinese officers learned, for the first time, that their passage would be disputed at West Point. Quite confident that whatever fiimsy defenses had been erected could be demolished by a few shots, they simply dropped their torpedo nettings, and steamed ahead.

West Point lies about half way between the cities of Peekskill and Newburgh. The river flows from north to south, and the tides extend to Albany. Going northward, and up the river (as the Chinese fleet was going) the river is not straight between Peekskill and Newburgh, but has four sharp turns each of which is almost a right angle. At Peekskill it takes an abrupt turn to the west, then quickly turns north again and narrows rapidly. Its banks here are wild and picturesque. On either side high hills slope abruptly down into the water. At West Point the river makes another sharp turn to the west and then almost immediately turns to the north again and flowing for a mile or two through a narrow pass widens out into a broad inland lake, on the western shore of which is the city of Newburgh. Just below the turn, at West Point, the river channel runs close to a sheer, unbroken precipice of rock which towers several hundred feet above the river, and on its western side. It was at this point that the Chinese met with their first loss of life.

It had been early morning when the Chinese naval detachment had left New York and it was now about sunset, but the detachment, contemptuous of the make-shift defenses it was to encounter, proceeded on its way, intending to anchor for the night off Newburgh. At quarter speed, it steamed slowly up the river from Peekskill, the torpedo boats preceding the armored cruisers, feeling their way cautiously for fear of torpedoes, and every now and then, exploding a torpedo in hope of unmasking whatever submarine mines there might be in the channel.

Already had the advance torpedo boat passed beneath the precipice of rock, of which I have previously spoken, and yet there had been no sign that the passage of the detachment would be disputed. But when the second torpedo boat came beneath the frowning wall, a score of human forms showed themselves on the summit and as many cans of dynamite and packages of gun-cotton fell through the air. There was a fusillade of detonations, followed almost immediately by a louder report. The water rose in a huge column skyward, and as it fell again a few shattered fragments were borne onward by the tide. One vessel of the invading fleet had been totally destroyed.

The armored cruisers stopped, rolled heavily for a minute or two, and then their ports opened and they began to shell the precipice. The height was, however, so great and the vessels were so close to its base, that the guns could not be given sufficient elevation to throw the shot to the summit, and it was necessary for the ships to drop a mile or so down the river before any raking or enfilading fire could be delivered over the summit. In the meantime the catapults and other hastily-erected engines had opened fire on the remaining torpedo boat, which endeavored to escape by retreating, passing over to the other side of the river to avoid again passing under the precipice that had proved so fatal to its companion. In its anxiety, however, to avoid the precipice, it came too close to the opposite shore, and, owing, probably, to the ignorance of its pilot, ran on a ledge of rock that here projects into the river. While there stationary, a masked battery of what were then called by the old Roman name of '*balistae*" and which were nothing more than "mechanical slings," which threw dynamite in a sort of guess-work fashion, with a range of about a quarter of a mile — a masked battery of these improvised and hastily-built machines — opened on it from behind the railroad track.

It was now quite late in the evening—probably about half-past-eight at night. The sun had long since disappeared over the western hills, but the night was clear, and though the moon had not yet risen the stars were bright and objects on the river were plainly discernible from the shore, while from the river the shore seemed one uniform mass of shadow. The armored cruisers still hung at anchor, their electric search-lights blazing through the clear air and their torpedo nettings down. But they had ceased all but an irregular discharge of their guns, for their search-lights, while they protected them from the approach of a foe, yet so blinded them that they could distinguish nothing beyond the circle of light. The torpedo boat, becoming each moment yet more fast aground — for the tide was falling — followed the example of its companion ships, and turned on its search-light. This was favorable to the Nationalists on shore, as it served them for a mark to fire at, while they were doubly protected by the darkness. Up to midnight, the Nationalists kept up a continual fusillade from their imperfect engines without effecting any damage upon their foes, while the ships returned a desultory fire that, owing to the uncertainty of aim, did little material damage. About one o' clock in the morning, however, a projectile happened luckily to strike the extreme stern end of the torpedo boat and, exploding, tore away the screw and rudder. [10] A few minutes after this shot, the boat displayed a white flag and the Nationalists putting out in a small boat received the surrender of the vessel. She was, however, rapidly filling with water and was practically a total wreck, but the Nationalists obtained from her what was of inestimable value, and that was some seven or eight score of the improved self-loading airguns with which the Chinese soldiers were armed, and of which there had not before been even one in the possession of the Americans. Some of these were retained by the Nationalists at West Point while the rest were forwarded to Chicago, whence they were distributed to various factories as models of what was wanted.

Deprived of the support of the torpedo boats, the two cruisers gave up the battle; and, taking advantage of the light of the rising moon, they turned about and steamed down the river.

This is what is known as the battle of West Point. It greatly encouraged the Nationalists and gave a certain credibility to the foolish idea that the ingenuity of a people was a complete defense in time of war. The victory was really due to the curious configuration of the river banks and to a concatenation of fortunate circumstances. It resulted, however, in checking the Chinese advance, and, as such, was of incalculable value to the Nationalists, giving them a chance to recover from the confusion of their first surprise.

Two days afterward, however (October 10th), the

Chinese vessels in the Hudson were reinforced by an additional cruiser and four thousand infantry soldiers; and a combined attack having then been made by the army and navy, West Point was easily captured.

*Chapter 9 LECTURE IX.*

These discourses are purely initiatory to the studies which will subsequently engross your attention, and hence my object is to present to you in a very cursory way a very general review of the events of the past decade, the weakness of the Nationalistic system, and also the general gloom and confusion which possessed men's minds when that system was tried and found wanting. It is in fulfillment of this last purpose that I have quoted so largely from the contemporaneous history of Professor West's diary. I now, therefore, quote from that source again. He says:

" At Springfield we received news of the bombardment of New York. The reports are conflicting—one especially, to my mind, bears intrinsic evidence of falsehood, since it declares that the Chinese war-ships can fire each of their guns only once a day. These reports, however, have come, I find, mostly by telephone from private sources, as no authoritative news has been posted since the Government News Bureau fled from Washington.

" It took us all day to get from Springfield to Albany ! This is the first sign (that I have noticed) that the social or governmental system has been disarranged by the arrival of the Chinese. The difficulties of our trip to Springfield were due to the invasion only because of the stoppage of trains at the Boston terminus, which though it affected many miles of road, might still be called only a local stoppage, since the train service to that city was not disturbed nor did it interfere with the working of the Nationalistic system in any of the interior towns. But the delay between Springfield to Albany was caused by a wholly unforeseen and unexpected increase in the passenger traffic, which the road was called on to accommodate, and for which no preparation had been made, nor estimate furnished beforehand.

" In the days of my youth, such blockings of traffic were not unusual, but the results were different. There was a certain freedom of action then, which enabled engineers and conductors and local railroad oflicials, somehow or other to work out a solution ; but under the Nationalistic system each man's duty was so exactly defined, that to go beyond its limits was treason, and though men had not yet been by it degraded into absolute machines, they had been brought near enough to that point to permit almost any unforeseen circumstance to cause a far-reaching derangement of the governmental system.

" Our journey from Boston to Springfield had been under such difficulties—arising from the entirely unprecedented way in which it was made — that my mind was wholly engrossed by the attendant anxieties; but our trip between Springfield and Albany was made in a passenger car, which though greatly overcrowded, was not wholly uncomfortable, and the length of time consumed by the journey afforded me an opportunity for reflection.

" In case this diary should hereafter be read by my children, I would not have them think, from what I have here set down, that I have formed the opinion that the ability of the individuals of to-day is less than it was in the days when I was young. I would not have them so understand, because that is not my belief. The railroad officials, whom I have come in contact with during our flight from Boston, have uniformly seemed to me to possess remarkable intellectual ability. But (in the privacy of this journal), I cannot flnd words strong enough to reprobate the system which has made them so thoroughly part of a governmental machine that they cannot use their individual ingenuity in the performance of their official duties. Truly, the wisest and best system of government is that which gives the greatest latitude of action to individuals and requires only that results shall be satisfactory and methods honest and upright.

" It seems very strange to me that I alone, of all the millions in this land, should have any thing like a just appreciation of war. It is true that I was but an infant when the war waged between the North and the South; but, even so, there was something then in the minds of all about me and in the common talk of my childhood's friends, that have made me wiser, as I think, than the men of the present generation — or if not wiser, perhaps more far-seeing. It seems to me as if I had learned long years ago, what the people of this nation are just beginning to learn. War is to them something so strange that even now, after the experience of the last few days, they look on the invasion as an incident of only a transient nature; and their eagerness to get news of what is going on seems to me rather the curiosity of children to hear of something which is new, than the desire of thoughtful men to obtain information on which they may base action. Nor will my judgment allow me to agree with those whom I have talked with, when they say that the invasion is a temporary thing and that the nation is too strong to be conquered. As for the aid of England and Germany, they are as helpless as we are, and I cannot see that they could aid us more than a tribe of negroes from Africa could in my day have aided

France in a war against Germany.

" Each day I recognize more and more how utterly helpless we must be against force. Without a single soldier, without a fort, or a ship of War, without fire-arms, without munitions of war, without one single factory that can turn out implements of war, what can we do against a well-armed and well-disciplined foe? That we will ultimately conquer, I have still faith enough in the race to believe; but I shudder when I think of the expenditure of human life that must ensue before the final victory is ours. Strange, indeed, that we should have been so intoxicated with pride in our material prosperity as not to see that it was ready to fall before the first armed nation that chose to attack us.

" I have said that our car was overcrowded. There was, in fact, quite an exodus from Springfield, west. Most of the passengers, however, were from New York. They had fled after the first day's bombardment, coming hither by way of New Haven and Hartford. Most of them were of middle age — men and women who were called my contemporaries — and who, having reached the age of forty-five, had been relieved from enforced labor and been at liberty to come and go as they saw fit. The discipline in which the younger active members of the industrial force had been reared had been too strict for any but those who had served their time to think of leaving without special orders from the government.

" Edith was in her element among these. She had always liked old people—partly, perhaps, because her aged father and mother had made her their companion, partly also, perhaps (as I used to say to her, jokingly), because she had a husband who, as ages were usually counted, was nigh on to two hundred years old. She shared the contents of our lunch baskets among those who had been less provident than ourselves, and even, from the recesses of one of our bundles of impedimenta, produced knitting-needles and a ball of yarn for one old dame who complained pathetically to her that the machinery of that feminine method of passing away the time had been forgotten in the hurry of departure.

"At Albany it was impossible for us to procure immediate transportation westward, and we found ourselves under the necessity of remaining there over night. To procure quarters, however, was by no means easy. The city was filled with fugitives, young and old, who had fled hither from New York and the river cities. We learned here, too, the terrible news of the destruction of New York and the progress of the Chinese fleet up the river. We heard, too, that some, sort of a defense was to be attempted at West Point, but what the nature of the defense was I could not learn, though the wildest rumors about it prevailed. I had in my youth spent many happy hours at West Point, and I can still remember some of the brave and gallant men I met there at the Military School. Alas there is no school there now! Where honor and bravery once ruled, fashion is now the sole mistress. Since my awakening I have not been to West Point, but I remember it well. Would to God that there could be found there now as in the old days, some Anderson, Harrison or Johnson, or some scion of the Greenes or Perrys, whose military skill and training would have sufficed to defend the post against the enemy.

" But these are idle wishes. The art of war has found no followers in these days when the arts of peace only have been worshipped. When I think that soon the sounds of battle will echo through the glades and from the hillsides of West Point, in my mind's eye I can almost see, a troop of shadows, ghosts of the heroic dead, flocking thither to defend the sacred soil from the dishonor of a foeman's tread. Alas, these are but idle dreams. The dead are far away from war's alarms, and no ghostly trumpet will echo defiance to the enemy's approach. But enough! There is work to do today that claims all my energies.

" It was impossible for us to find accommodation in any of the public inns at Albany, and we might have fared badly had not some of the acquaintances that we had made on the train come to our aid and found us lodgings among their acquaintances at Albany.

" The news that we had received determined me to make a change in my plans. Instead of leaving Edith and the children in the Adirondacks and re-turning myself to Boston, as had hitherto been my intention, I determined to go with them still further westward and, if possible, reach Chicage. I can clearly foresee that this invasion is not to be the thing of a day, but that years of war will ensue. If these prognostications are correct, the post of duty, as well as of honor, will be in the army. From the rumors I hear of what has happened at Boston, Shawmut College is a thing of the past; to return there would consequently be as useless as 'twould be foolish. To go to Chicago seems the wisest course.

" All day of the 7th was spent by me in vain endeavor to procure transportation westward. It was easy enough to buy tickets, but when the time came for our train to leave, so many wished to take it that a great crowd was around the station — so great and densely packed that I was afraid to have Edith and the children become part of it — and, therefore, we lost the day. I knew that special trains were leaving, bat could find no one who could teU me how to procure passage on them. That night, however, Leete asked me to let him try, and on receiving my permission, asked me for our tickets and begged the loan of my credit card, as his was nearly exhausted. I gave it to him, of course, and he started off happy, but his request set me thinking. The credit allowed us by the government was, indeed, large enough for all ordinary occasions, and of course, no extraordinary event, such as war, had been contemplated when the amount was fixed — but the extraordinary event had come to pass just the same. I remember there used to be a saying in my youth to the effect that 'it is the unexpected that always happens.' Here, also, was another weakness in the Nationalistic system, in that it permitted no one to provide, by frugality and accumulation, for any future, unforeseen or unexpected event. Accumulations of credit were permitted only when the purpose to which the accumulation was to be devoted was explained to the authorities and approved of by them — and it is needless to record that the circumstances now surrounding us had not been foreseen; nor, had they been imagined by me, would they have been accepted by the authorities as a valid reason for an accumulation. True, some provision had been made by which allowances could be increased, but the granting of such an increase necessitated so much red tape and consumed so much time that the provision was practically useless in such an emergency as the present. Fortunately we had until the first of the year in which to spend our credits, and fortunately, also, we had been unusually economical up to the time of our departure from Boston, so that we still had nearly half a year's credits at our disposal. We would have been in an extremely bad predicament had it been otherwise.

" About one o'clock, on the morning of the 8th, Leete came to my room and, waking me, announced that he had procured transportation for us on a special train leaving at four o'clock. I questioned him somewhat as to how he had succeeded, but as his answers were short and somewhat evasive, I saw that he did not care to tell me, and so did not press him.

" Although our train did not leave until four, Leete told me that it was advisable that we should be at the station as much earlier as possible, so having dressed I sallied out and collected my family from the various friends who had given them shelter. This consumed two hours, so that it was after three when we at last reached the station. Leete showed his pass to a door-keeper, who passed us through the gates. The train was of sleeping-cars and a little more than half filled, but we managed to find comfortable quarters near to each other. Before we left, however, the train became crowded, and we were forced to pack ourselves more closely than we had at first expected.

" When Leete returned my credit card I found the

amount punched from it smaller than I expected —indeed I understood it was no more than we would have had to pay six months ago — but later I noticed that a very handsorne pair of jewelled cuff-buttons which Leete had been wearing had been replaced by a very cheap pair, and upon persistent questioning he told me, after I had promised that his communication should be secret, that he had presented them to the division Superintendent in order to secure our passage. He had learned, he said, that train accommodation was given as a matter of favor, and while he was talking to the Superintendent and ofEering to pay double and even treble rates of fare, the Superintendent admired the cuff-buttons, 'and then,' said Leete, 'I took them off and asked him to accept them, which he did, and a few minutes afterward he made out our pass and gave it to me.'

" I thought to myself, as Leete told me his tale, that human nature was not now much changed from what it had been a century and a half ago, and I remembered to have heard that an era of official corruption began with and followed after the war of 1861. I wonder if the invasion of the Chinese has begun a similar era, or if Leete's experience is an isolated instance of the depravity of human nature ?

" We reached Chicago on the 10th, after a slow but not uncomfortable journey. Our first occupation was, of course, to procure accommodations, which we succeeded at last in doing, finding them in the home of two ancient maiden ladies of the name of Shacklefurd. My next care was to have our cards of credit extended, and for this purpose I went to seek for information as to the proper officer to apply to."

Professor West in his diary gives a lengthy and detailed account of his wanderings about Chicago when he endeavored to find some person who could provide him an advance of credit. His eldest son, Leete, was occupied in the same attempt, and was especially anxious to succeed quickly, as his departure for Boston was necessarily delayed while his credit was exhausted.

I have preferred for the sake of condensation to omit this portion of Professor West's diary. I must, however, invite your attention to the fact that this credit system went down under the press of war. It had been one of the pet theories of the Nationalists, and in time of peace had unquestionably worked well, but being absolutely unelastic and by discouraging saving habits on the part of citizens, and, indeed, forbidding men to provide against unforeseen contingencies, it worked, now, great injury to citizens.

This point is so important that I venture to repeat for your benefit what was said on the subject by Dr. Leete. I quote from " *Looking Backward*," Chapter XIX:

" A credit corresponding to his share of the annual product of the nation is given to every citizen on the public books at the beginning of each year, and a credit card issued him with which he procures at the public storehouses, found in every community, whatever he desires whenever he desires it. This arrangement, you will see, totally obviates the necessity for business transactions of any sort between individuals and consumers. Perhaps, you would like to see what our credit cards are like.

" You observe," he pursued, as I was curiously examining the piece of pasteboard he gave me, "that this card is issued for a

104

certain number of dollars. We have kept the old word but not the substance. The term, as we use it, answers to no real thing, but merely serves as an algebraical symbol for comparing the values of products with one another. For this purpose they are all priced in dollars and cents just as in your day. The value of what I procure on this card is checked off by the clerk, who pricks out of these tiers of squares the price of what I order."

" If you wanted to buy something of your neighbor could you transfer part of your credit to him as consideration ? " I inquired.

" In the first place," replied Dr. Leete, " our neighbors have nothing to sell to us, but in any event our credit would not be transferable, being strictly personal. Before the nation could even think of honoring any such transfer as you speak of it would be bound to inquire into all the circumstances of the transaction, so as to be able to guarantee its absolute equity. It would have been reason enough, had there been no other, for abolishing money, that its possession was no indication of rightful title to it. In the hands of the man who had stolen it or murdered for it, it was as good as in those which had earned it by industry. People nowadays interchange gifts and favors out of friendship, but buying and selling is considered absolutely inconsistent with the mutual benevolence and disinterestedness which should prevail between citizens, and the sense of community which supports our social system. According to our ideas, buying and selling is essentially anti-social in all its tendencies. It is an education in self-seeking at the expense of others, and no society, whose citizens are trained in such a school, can possibly rise above a very low grade of civilization."

" What if you have to spend more than your card in any one year ?" I asked.

" The provision is so ample that we are more likely not to spend it all," replied Dr. Leete. "But if extraordinary expenses should exhaust it, we can obtain a limited advance on the next year's credit, though this practice is not encouraged and a heavy discount is charged to check it."

"If you don't spend your allowance I suppose it accumulates?"

" That is also permitted to a certain extent, where a special outlay is anticipated. But unless notice to the contrary is given, it is presumed that the citizen who does not fully expend his credit did not have occasion to do so and the balance is turned into the general surplus."

" Such a system does not encourage saving habits on the part of citizens," I said.

" It is not intended to," was the reply.

" The nation is rich, and does not wish the people. to deprive themselves of any good thing. In your day, men were bound to lay up goods and money against coming failure of the means of support and or their children. This necessity made parsimony a virtue. But now it would have no such laudable object, and having lost its utility it has ceased to be regarded as a virtue. No man any more has any care for the morrow, either for himself or his children, for the nation guarantees the nurture, education and comfortable maintenance of every citizen from the cradle to the grave."

The fallacy of this specious reasoning had passed unnoticed by the people until suddenly (but not without warning) the National guarantee "of comfortable maintenance of every citizen, from the cradle to the grave," became worthless. Millions of people found themselves penniless among strangers, and through no fault of their own. Those who remained in the cities were penniless, because they were not able to persuade a Frenchman or a Chinese that the privilege of punching a hole in their credit cards was a valuable return for food, clothing or shelter. Those who fled from the cities, found their credit cards exhausted by the expenses of their flight and were unable to procure the necessities of life, because they had no cards to be punched. As credit cards were not transferable there was no way in which the refugees from the cities could obtain new credits except through the proper officers, and in the endeavor to find that proper officer millions of people had, no doubt, the same experiences that Professor West had. In other words, their search resulted only in failure.

There was in fact no official in Chicago who had legally the right to grant an increase of credit to any citizen of Boston or New York, or indeed to any one not a citizen of Chicago. Credit was a matter of book-keeping. A regular routine had to be followed, and that routine had to be the same in every portion of the country. The person desiring an increase of credit, first filled in and signed a blank application. This had then to be approved by the local Superintendent of his guild or trade, who afterward forwarded it to the head of that trade, who having approved of it, sent it on to the proper officer at Washington. If this last-named official also approved, he so notified the head of the credit card department at Washington, who thereupon caused cards for the desired amount to be made and sent to the disbursing agent at the place of application, from whom the applicant could then receive them.

It will be at once perceived that under this system it was now impossible for the refugees from Boston to obtain an increase of credit in Chicago.

The Wests fared better than many less-known people. Professor West's public position and strange experience had made him famous. When citizens from Chicago had visited Boston, they had been anxious to see and speak to him. In this way many persons had made his acquaintance and, now, these united to entertain his family. They would gladly have transferred to him portions of their own credit cards, but their credit was not transferable, being strictly personal. But by sleeping first at one house, and then at another, and by dining for stated intervals, first with one friend and then with another, the Wests did not actually suffer.

This method of hospitality was very generally exercised in all the inland towns, and thus the refugees from the coast cities were provided, more or less plentifully, with the necessities of life. There was, however, much suffering among those whose flight had exhausted their credit cards.

## Chapter 10 LECTURE X.

" I had been two days in Chicago," says Professor West, "two busy days consumed wholly in arranging for the comfort of my family — but on the third day, the most pressing of our personal matters having been attended to, it occurred to me, that it was my duty as an officer of the government, to pay my respects to the President.

" The house now used as the presidential mansion was a large and commodious building fronting on Lincoln Park, and thither I took my way. On my arrival there and on the presentation of my card, one of the President's Secretaries came to me. The President, he said, was in, but was just now engaged with some of the Chiefs of the great divisions. That he would wish to see me, the Secretary was kind enough to say, was beyond doubt. My card would be at once sent to him, and if I would wait a little while until he was at leisure, I should confer a favor. Of course, I waited.

" After an interval of probably a quarter of an hour, I was told that the President would receive me, and following my guide, was soon in the Executive chamber. There were several Chiefs of the divisions present, and after mutual introductions had passed and we were all seated, the President said to me:

" 'I am indeed glad that you have called, Professor. "We were deliberating on public affairs when your card was brought in, and it immediately occurred to us all, that it would be beneficial to learn from you what steps would probably have been taken by the government, as it existed in your youth, had such contingencies as embarrass us to-day, then occurred.'

" ' What,' I exclaimed, ' have no measures been taken to save the country ?'

"' Oh, most certainly,' he answered. ' The government statisticians have been hard at work calculating the increased production which the seizure of the coast cities will necessitate. Congress, you know, will meet on the 20th, and I intend then to recommend that the hours of labor be lengthened and probably that the workers who are about to retire be retained a year or two longer. There will be also submitted a proposition to reduce the allowance made to each individual; and thus by an increase of production, and a decrease of consumption we hope to prevent the industries of the nation from being permanently disorganized. This calling of a special session of Congress was a very radical step on my part, but I have no doubt that the people will consider it justified by the exigencies of the occasion.

It is my purpose also, as soon as this special session adjourns *sine die*, to call another session of Congress.

"' But,' said I, in great wonderment, ' why these two sessions — these two Congresses ?'

" The President smiled and shook his head at me. ' I will convince you by your own words,' he said, and he went to a book case and took down the volume I had written nearly a score of years ago and which I called *Looking Backward.*

"He turned over the pages hastily till he came to the place he sought. ' See,' he said, ' here are your own words — here is what you have written in the nineteenth chapter. Let me read it to you : ' But with no state legislature, and Congress meeting only once in five years, how do you get you legislation done?' 'We have no legislation,' replied Dr. Leeie, 'that is next to none. It is rarely that Congress even when it meets considers any new laws of consequence, and then it has only power to commend them to the followvng Congress, lest any thing he done hastily. If you will consider a moment, Mr. West, you will see that we have nothing to make laws about. "

" ' Those are Dr. Leete's words, not mine!' I protested.

"'They are a correct statement of the constitutional powers of Congress,' answered the President. ' You see now why I wish to call the two sessions of Congress. The question whether the second session of Congress will be so far a second Congress as to enable tbe recommended laws which they pass to be legally laws is now under the consideration of the Cabinet. In the mean time myself and the Chiefs of the Divisions have exercised powers that are, at least, of doubtful constitutionality (but I trust the people will pardon us), for we hope that by so doing we have prevented the industries of the country from being seriously disorganized.'

"I confess that I listened with astonishment. While it was true, of course, that the production and distribution of the necessities of life, food, clothing and the like, were of great importance — and while the invasion of the Chinese was likely to increase the difficulties, not only of production, but especially of distribution — were there not questions of greater importance, questions of National defense? I expressed something of this thought to the President.

" 'Yes,' he said, 'there has been some talk about that. What would the government have done in your youth, Professor ?'

"' An extra session of Congress would have been called at once ('That we have done,' interpolated the President); the regular army would have been concentrated at points most likely to check the advance of the enemy and to afford nuclei around which the State militia could be gathered. The President would have called for volunteers, and the Secretary of War would have purchased arms, ammunition, clothing, etc. In short, the government in the days of my youth, would have done exactly the reverse from what I understand you have done. They would have put aside all economic questions until Congress should meet, and devote themselves wholly to military affairs.'

"' Had your government, then, such extraordinary authority?' exclaimed the President. 'Not even for the best ends would we allow our rulers such powers.'

"Then I remembered what had before been blotted from my memory by the lapse of years—I remembered that on the first day of my awakening. Dr. Leete had told me that the government had no war powers. [11]

" ' But,' said I, ' it seems incredible, that with an invader not only at your gates but on your soil, with your liberties not only threatened, but with millions of the people in captivity (for in what other state can the inhabitants of the coast cities be said to be) — it seems to me incredible that in these circumstances no steps have been taken to create an army — to meet force by force. You tell me that your powers are limited, and that it would be treason to assume such vast authority. But what limits your authority ? — the Constitution. But what is the object of tfie Constitution ? Is not its sole purpose to secure the lives, liberties and happiness of the people ? How then in fulfilling the plain purpose of the Constitution do you override it ? If to now assume war powers sufficient to call for volunteers, to bid the people arrn and muster for national defense — if this be treason, then it is a grand and glorious treason for which you would deserve the everlasting gratitude of the nation.'

"The President shook his head. 'You reason eloquently, Professor,' he said,' but you will pardon me if I say that I fear you do not reason correctly. Do you realize that what you ask me to do is to seize upon the bodies of citizens and deliver them over by hundreds of thousands to death and mutilation ? What right have I — what constitutional or moral right have I, to sacrifice the life of one man, even to save the lives of ten others ?'

" ' Perhaps,' said I, ' if there be no authority for the exercise, by the Executive, of such powers as the occasion calls for, there may be found authority for a part of such powers. These powers, moreover, once belonged to the presidential office; perhaps, in their repeal there may be some deficiency or defect which may enable the President to act partially as the occasion requires. It used to be said, in the days when I was young, that there was no law that a lawyer drew, but what some shrewder lawyer could find a defect in it.'

" A very desultory conversation ensued, in the midst of which luncheon was announced, and I being invited to join the President and the Cabinet at this meal, we all proceeded to the dining-room of the mansion.

" Afterward, we returned to the Executive chamber and resumed our conversation. Here we were shortly afterward joined by the remainder of the chiefs of the ten grand divisions of the industrial army, who had been absent during our previous discussions, but who (as I subsequently learned) had been sent for by the President. For their benefit the President hastily summarized the conversation that had already taken place. He then asked me to specify, more in detail, what power I considered most important to be exercised in the present emergency.

" 'Any power or powers,' said I, ' that will result in collecting men for an army and disciplining them into an army — powers that can authorize the production and accumulation of powder and shot and fire-arms, uniforms and rations for the soldiers, and generally, all munitions of war. Who, for example, disposes of the workers in the unclassified grade? "What is Muster Day, that is now almost here ? And when the apprentices have served for the year now ending, who determines what grades they shall be enrolled in? Of course, practically this must be done by the individual's immediate superior — but in whose name is it done ? Is it not done nominally by the central government ?'

" 'If then,' I continued, 'under the Nationalistic theory that the President is the Commander-in-chief of the industrial army — so closely allied to them that the workers are actually prohibited from voting for him, or having any voice in his selection — has he not power to select from them men to meet an unexpected, but pressing demand ? Has not the President power on the next Muster Day to designate the army as the branch of the industrial service most in need of service? It seems to me, that in the power, theoretically possessed, if not ordinarily exercised, by the President, there can be found means to collect soldiers and to form an army. And what is the demand for guns and uniforms and powder and shot, but a demand by every individual in the nation for the production of those articles ? Had the people demanded a new variety of silk, or some new kind of cotton cloth, would you not order its manufacture? Would you wait for the quiennial session of Congress to authorize its manufacture? How does the manufacture of munitions of war differ in principle from the manufacture of silk or cotton ? It seems to me, that the powers already exercised by the government — or a very slight extension of them — are sufficient to authorize, at least, the beginnings of an army.'

" So, we talked until late in the afternoon ; and then I took my leave.

" On my return to our lodgings I found Edith curious to

know why I had not returned for luncheon and full of all the news that a day's gossiping still gave to the gentler sex. I can remember when I was a boy, hearing my father tease my mother's female friends about woman's propensity to gad here and there and get the news. I tease Edith in somewhat the same way now and then, but, nevertheless, I usually listen to what she has to say. So that night, when I reached our lodgings and heard that she had a budget of news to unfold to me, I made some humorously sarcastic remarks which made her laugh and all the more eager to impart her news to me.

" The next morning, before we had breakfasted, I received a note from the President asking me to call at the Executive mansion at ten o'clock. I was there at the appointed hour, and was immediately ushered to ihe President. He at once disclosed his object in sending for me.

"' Professor,' he said, ' we have determined to appoint five Commissioners to meet an equal number of Commissioners from the Chinese, and I wish you to be one of them.'

"I at once answered that my time was at my country's disposal, but I questioned if my abilities were equal to the occasion. To this he replied that I was the only one who had doubts on that subject, and that the Cabinet when my name had been mentioned were unanimous about my fitness for the position. I then inquired what our duties were to be and what powers we would have.

" ' On those points,' said the President, ' I can hardly say any thing definite. My instructions to you must be of the most general kind. The largest latitude will be allowed you. Until late last night we discussed, what had been the subject of our afternoon's conversation, the powers of the Executive. I regret to say that we were forced to conclude that the President had no war powers such as you described as belonging to the Executive in the nineteenth century. I cannot, therefore, empower you to negotiate any final treaty with our invaders. You are rather to remonstrate with them on the invasion of the country and especially upon the wanton destruction of life and property in Boston and New York. It is our wish that the Commissioners should, however, procure from our invaders the general substance of such a treaty as would be acceptable to them and to discuss generally the situation that it may be reported by them to Congress. You will remonstrate, also, in the strongest possible terms, on the unheard-of cruelty of deporting the populations of our maritime cities and I say now to you privately, that I am sure Congress will listen to no adjustment of the present difficulty that does not contemplate the immediate return of these unfortunate exiles. It is important also that some arrangement be made by which the credit cards of those of our people in the cities occupied by the enemy be continued good for the purchase of the necessities of life, and that the Nationalistic system of distributing the products of the country be at once resumed. These are the general matters which the Commissioners will discuss and report upon, so that Congress may be able to act advisedly. Other subjects will undoubtedly occur to you, and, as I said, the greatest latitude of discussion will be allowed you.'

" I listened attentively while the President thus explained

his purpose. When he had finished, I said to him :

" ' I had much rather, sir, that you would give me authority to raise and equip a regiment, or even a brigade. I know nothing of the science of war, but I am sure that I would receive far more respectful terms from the Chinese if I came to them as the leader of what called itself an army, than I shall when I go as Commissioner of these United States however great and powerful we are commercially. Force must be met by force—not by words.

"' You do not then approve of the plan ?' broke in the President in a tone of surprise.

"' I cannot say that I disapprove of it,' I responded, 'for I cannot see what harm can result from it. But what I do greatly regret is that you should rely upon it wholly and exclusively.'

"' I think,' answered the President, ' that you fail to appreciate the immense power of international opinion. There is not a civilized nation in the world but what will hasten, to condemn the barbarous proceedings of the Chinese. We are, it is true, cut off from cable communication with the rest of the world, but I cannot doubt that already the very strongest remonstrances have been made by the other nations to the Chinese. These naturally must result in our favor.'

" ' If,' said I, ' other nations could oppose something besides words to the Chinese, then remonstrances might avail us something. But they are even more helpless than we are to do aught but talk. For centuries the Chinese have cared nothing for the opinions of the world, and the only rights that foreigners ever had in China were those which had been forcibly obtained by war. I cannot believe that now, suddenly, contrary to all the history of the race, the Chinese will for one moment yield to moral suasion, or to any thing but superior force, I speak my mind freely, but I trust that I do not offend.'

"' You certainly do not offend,' replied the President, ' but I could wish that you agreed with us. To me it seems that the age of force is past, and that the present era is wholly under the influence of moral ideas. But should you be right, it still is important that you should serve your country as a Commissioner, for should the Chinese refuse to listen to our remonstrances, it will then be necessary for us to purchase their retreat, and it will then become the duty of the Commissioners to fix the amount and times of payment of whatever ransom we may have to pay.'

"' Alas, Mr. President,' said I, ' I am still forced to disagree with you. Why should the Chinese accept a ransom when, by persisting, all that is ours will inevitably become theirs ? If a highwayman has knocked me down and robbed me of my purse, do you think that he would listen to my request to give me back half its contents? I realize now as never before that my ideas are not the ideas of my companions. I belong to another age. Pray, sir, permit me to decline the position you would appoint me to.'

" ' Not so, Professor,' the President quickly responded. '

If all other arguments fail, I must appeal to your love for your fellow-beings. Oh, Professor, Professor' (and I saw tears come now into his eyes), ' my heart bleeds at the thought of the sorrows and sufferings of our unhappy people in our coast cities. We can hear nothing but the most heartrending rumors of their condition, but as Commissioner you will, perhaps, be able to see them, talk with them and console them. For their sakes, I ask you not to refuse this appointment.'

" What answer could I make to such an appeal as this ? None, but to accept the duties of a Commissioner."

# Chapter 11 LECTURE XI.

"I then spoke to the President," continues Professor West, in his diary, "of my impecunious position, representing to him the reason of its existence, and mentioning my futile efforts to obtain an advance or addition of credit. He remarked thai the question of the expenses of the Commission had not occurred to him, but that he would at-once personally see that it was attended to, and summoning a messenger sent a request to the head of the General of the Credit Card Department to join us at once.

" Of course, I recognized that it was not the duty of the President to attend to the numerous details consequent upon the departure of the Commissioners, whether those details were the payment of their expenses, or the railway schedule of their transportation ; but, as I have already recorded, I had been unable to procure an extension of our family credit, and I was unwilling to leave Edith and the children dependent upon what, though disguised as the kindness of friends, we all recognized as charity. I was, therefore, glad to have our credit extended before my departure, even though that consummation required the personal interposition of the President.

" I oflEered to leave his Excellency to attend to his other business while I waited in the ante-room the arrival of the General of the Credit Card Department, but he bade me stay with him. My presence, he was kind enough to say, was a relief to him.

"' I am very weary of the burden of office,' he said. ' My responsibilities seem greater than I can bear. In the last week I have not averaged each day four hours of slumber. I dare not go to bed, for in my dreams I see millions of helpless people crying to me for help — help that neither I nor any one else know how to give. I catch my sleep, here, as chance lets me, between the visits of people I must see, and the pressure of business that must be attended to. My Secretaries have orders never to let me sleep longer than fifteen minutes at a time, for if I do, then dreams come to me. I dreamed the other night that I was a switchman on a railroad (you know I belonged to the railroad division of the industrial army). I had opened the switch to shunt a freight train on to a side track, and, then, suddenly, my limbs were paralyzed. I saw a passenger train rushing down the track. I knew that if that switch were not closed, and there was no one near to close it but myself, an awful accident would happen, and hundreds of people killed. But my arms and legs were paralyzed; I could not move. I tried to cry, out, but I could make no sound. Fortunately, at that moment, one of my Secretaries awoke me, but I shall never forget the awful mental agony of that dream. I had slept then over an hour. It was after that experience that I gave the order that I should never be allowed to sleep longer than fifteen minutes at a time.

" This personal anecdote — or, I might, perhaps, more properly call it confession — of the President, has led me to appreciate, in an entirely new light, the difficulties that beset the rulers of our nation.

" I stayed, therefore, with the President, and tried to

relieve his mind by telling, in as humorous a manner as possible, my journeys from pillar to post, while trying to get an advance of credit. I had succeeded in making the President laugh, when Mr. John Dennison, Chief of the Credit Card Department, arrived. The President explained to him what was wanted, and he at once said that he would immediately have cards for a year's credit made out and sent to me. At the President's suggestion, I agreed to await these cards at the presidential mansion.

' " No sooner had Mr. Dennison taken his leave than I bethought myself of Leete's anxiety to return to Boston. I told the President of it.

" ' It would never do to stand in the way of lovers,' he said with a smile, 'you and I must devise some solution for their difficulties.' He reflected for a moment, then said, ' I see no reason why the Commissioners should not be allowed to take a Secretary with them. What do you say to my appointing Leete to that post ? It will at least afford him safe conduct into and out of Boston, and you must arrange with the other Commissioners that he has sufficient leisure to see his sweetheart.' He sat down and wrote a few lines, then touched a bell, and said to the Secretary who came in response, ' Send some one at once with that to General Slocum [Lewis M. Slocum, Chief of the Railroad Department]; see that the commission is made out immediately, and then let some one have it at the Commissioners' train, so that Mr. West can receive it before the train leaves.'

"' Might I ask, Mr. President,' I said ' that a messenger be sent to my son, telling him to be at the depot in time to catch the train ?'

"' A very, happy suggestion,' replied his Excellency. And he gave orders accordingly.

" I remained with the President until a messenger came with the promised credit cards, then having thanked his Excellency for his many kindnesses, I took my departure.

" I had but little time left at my own disposal, for a special train on the Michigan Southern was to leave that afternoon at two o'clock, to take us to Albany, where it had been already arranged that we should meet Commissioners from the commanders of the fleets at Boston, New York and Washington. There was barely time for me to hurry to our lodgings, distribute the credit cards, tell Edith and Leete what had taken place, pack my gripsack, lunch and say good-bye to my family, and then catch the train. At my request Edith gave me half of the gold coin we had carried with us; and of this, Leete and I each secreted a half about our persons.

" The road was cleared for us, and we reached Albany the next day about noon. The first thing that struck me on our arrival at the city that had once been the capital of the great State of New York, was the different aspect which the city now presented from what it showed to us when we passed through it only a few days before. Then, as I have said, it was overcrowded and almost feverish in the activity of its denizens; now all who could forsake it had fled, and the numbness of fear was upon it.

" We were met at the station by a body of Chinese troops, and by them escorted through almost deserted streets to the municipal building, where the Chinese awaited us. I know not how the others felt, but for myself, looking now backward and seeking to recall the sensations that then visited me, the scene is implanted in my memory is one of the saddest that can be imagined. Once in a while, a curious face appeared at a window along the line of our march, to disappear again almost immediately, but there were no crowds in the streets we traversed, and the city seemed strangely silent.

" When, some score of years ago, I was awakened by Dr. Leete to a new age, and I might almost say to a new world, it took me some time to become accustomed to my surroundings, and especially to those manifestations of curiosity which my appearance in a new circle always occasioned. My story, however, soon became a twice-told tale to the Bostonians, and at last it was only at rare intervals that I was reminded that I was different from my associates. Now, however, the curiosity which the Chinese evinced whenever I appeared, recalled the sensations of my first awakening. My story was evidently known to them, and no doubt I was a great curiosity in their eyes. But my strange experience did not make me contemptible in their opinion; on the contrary they thought more of me than of my associates. Ancestors and the men of antiquity had been so long objects of veneration in the Celestial Empire, that I, who had been a contemporary with their progenitors seemed in their opinion to be entitled to the same respect that they entertained for those progenitors. They listened to me, therefore, as if the accumulated wisdom of two centuries spoke in my words.

" The Chinese Commissioners were men of high breeding and great intellectual attainments. Their polished manners, and skill in conversation (they all spoke excellent English) would have made them charming hosts, under different circumstances. As it was, they rendered the labors of the Commissioners less tedious than they otherwise would have been.

" We began by complying with our instructions, and remonstrating on the invasion. To this they answered that the proselyting attempted in China by the Nationalists made the invasion a matter of self-protection. To our remonstrance on the destruction of life and property in New York and Boston they answered that it had been a necessity occasioned by the riotous behavior of the Bostonians and by the attempted defense of New York. As for the deportation of United States citizens they defended it only on the ground of policy, declaring that it was true wisdom to decrease the number of opponents and afford place for their own fellow-citizens. They laughed to scorn any proposal to recognize the credit cards of the nation unless an equal sum in gold was placed with them as a collateral for their redemption.

" Our negotiations, however, were not begun and ended in a day; and when we had presented the Nationalistic demands and they had been formulated into the proper shape, the Chinese Commissioners notified us that before rendering any decisive answer they must communicate with the Admirals of the several fleets. This, they said, would take time — probably a week would elapse before an authoritative answer could be given—and having learned from our conversation that we were relying almost wholly on chance information as to the condition of the cities which they had conquered, they suggested that we spend the interval in visiting those cities and with our own eyes viewing the changes that had taken place. We telegraphed to Chicago and promptly received instructions to go; and so, with the understanding that we were to meet at Albany one week hence, we divided ; two of my associates went to Washington, two to New York, and Leete and I accompanied Commissioner Hi to Boston.

" A special train took us speedily to our destination, where we arrived on the morning of the 18th. The Admiral still made his headquarters on board ship, and thither we at once proceeded. Without delay, I was at once introduced to him, and both Commissioner Hi, Leete and myself were invited to breakfast with him. That meal ended, however, I was informed that Lieutenant Hi would be closeted with the Admiral during the day, and would not be able to accompany me about town, but I was introduced to Captain Lee, who, I was told, would be my host and cicerone during my stay. Accompanied by the Captain, whom I found to be an agreeable gentleman (as indeed were all the Chinese officers that I met), and having given my promise to the Admiral that I would refrain from fomenting, encouraging or advising rebellion, I sallied forth.

" There was less change in the aspect of the city than I had expected. There were fewer stragglers m the streets than usual — indeed, I learned that all whose business did not require them to be abroad were required to stay at home. The main streets were patroled by soldiers, who saluted my conductor (who was in the full uniform of his rank), and looked curiously at me. We took our way to the Municipal Building, where the Council were still prisoners, and which was still the place from which municipal aflfairs were directed. I was permitted to see these unfortunate gentlemen, who composed the Council, and to converse with them, but only, however, in the presence of Captain Lee. They hailed my arrival with joy, as one from that outside world from which they were secluded, but Captain Lee had warned me that they had been purposely kept in ignorance of all that had transpired outside of Boston since the 4th, and had requested me not to give them information on this point. To all their questions I was, therefore, unable to give an answer, while they in turn could tell me little of what had transpired in the city. I left them with regret; and then, at my request, went to the house that but so short time ago had been my home. It had been turned into a barrack for the soldiery, and had been sacked and dismantled. It was like home no longer, and weary and disheartened by what I had seen, I begged the Captain to take me back to his ship.

" It was five o'clock when we reached the ship, and I was at once shown to my apartment — a room adjoining the Captain's, and as luxuriously fitted with all the conveniences as a stateroom in a private yacht would have been in my youth. A bath refreshed me greatly, and a cup of excellent tea subsequently partaken of in the Captain's cabin made me feel quite myself again. At seven we dined with the Admiral, and I met the commanders of the ships then in the harbor. After dinner, most of the superior officers of the Chinese service dropped in, evidently in consequence of a previous invitation, and the cabin was quite crowded. I did not at first realize that I was the attraction they had come to see, but when one or two had politely asked me questions about naval affairs and discipline in the nineteenth century, I realized the fact that 1 was as great a curiosity to these highly-educated gentlemen as I had been a few hours previously to the common soldiers, and many years ago to Dr Leete and his contemporaries.

" When, about midnight, the guests had all departed, and the Captain and I and a couple of the junior officers of the ship were left alone, I ventured to speak of what I had noticed.

"' Yes,' he said, ' we have heard in China of your wonderful experiences, and it is not strange that we should be anxious to see an individual who represents the highest type of the civilization of two centuries. It is a favorite matter of discussion with us, whether the civilization of this country was higher in the nineteenth century than it is to-day. Our best thinkers are by no means agreed on the answer and it would be interesting to know what your opinion is after a practical experience in both.'

"' I have no hesitation in answering at once,' I said, ' that the civilization of to-day is vastly higher than that of the nineteenth century, with the sole exception of the power of self-defense. In the days of my youth you would not so easily have conquered us; but I am not so sure,' I added, ' that we will not under our present civilization develop powers of resistance and retaliation which will astonish the world.'

" We sat talking for an hour or so longer and then retired.

" The next morning while breakfasting the Captain noticed me examining the paintings which decorated the walls of his cabin, and spoke of it.

"' Yes,' said I, ' in the nineteenth century the cabins of our war-ships were not usually galleries of fine arts. But it seems to me that I have seen most of these paintings before, so that it may be that they are recent acquisitions ?'

"' They are,' said Captain Lee. ' They were part of the collection of the Bassetts, and were purchased by me only a day or two ago. Oil paintings by master hands are no more now than in your early days, part of the furnishings of a war-ship. Though of course then as now the commanding officer may decorate his cabin as he chooses, provided of course that he does not interfere with the working power of the ship.'

" I need not record here the details of my observations in Boston, as I have noted them on a separate paper from which my report to the President and Congress will be drafted. Suffice to say that while I saw much that compelled me to admire the ingenuity with which our invaders have made the main features of our Nationalistic theory serve the ends of their own government, I saw also much that caused me great grief in the apathy of our citizens and the debasement which had already begun to show in society, I reserve all comments on this subject, however, for my report. I was not sorry, however, when the time came for me to return to Albany with Commissioner Hi."

## Chapter 12 LECTURE XII.

Among the many papers which have come into my possession, there is one, the authorship of which is anonymous. I have myself, however, no doubt whatsoever, but that it was written by Bartlett Leete West, owing to the fact that the Wests have always remained within the Nationalist lines, and to the circumstance that no opportunity has hitherto occurred by which I could get Colonel West's admission that he wrote it, its authorship still remains in doubt.[12]

Leete West had been placed under the escort of one of the junior lieutenants of the flagship. I may here remark, that the object of thus guarding himself and his father, was not to prevent them from associating with their friends, or in any way to circumscribe their liberty. It was solely for their protection. Few of the soldiers who sentineled the city could understand English, and the Wests, if unescorted, might have been subject to annoyance or insult by these soldiers. Wherever Leete West went, therefore. Lieutenant Wong, as a matter of precaution, was ordered to go also.

Mr. West has since risen to be a distinguished officer in the military service of the Nationalist government. It gives me pleasure to state that the unanimous testimony of all of my countrymen whom he met, while in Boston as Secretary of the Commissioners, is that he was then one of the most agreeable and fascinating young men they had ever met. He won the hearts of nearly all the officers of the fleet, from the Admiral down to the midshipmen, and when his love affair became known there was not one Chinese officer, but what wished him a successful culmination to it. He must have had much of that same charm and fascination of manner that history tells us was possessed to so great a degree by that distinguished editor of the nineteenth century, Allen Thorndike Rice.

This manuscript which I have referred to, and from which I am about to quote is partly written in cipher. It is apparently an account of Mr. West's doings in Boston, and is a purely personal narrative. I invite your attention to it, not because of its literary merit, nor because the progress of Mr. West's love affair in any way falls within the scope of these lectures, but because it partially describes the habits and thoughts of a representative Boston family of that period.

It was not until the day after his arrival in Boston, that Leete West was at leisure to seek his sweetheart. The manuscript recites his impatience at the delay, and continues:

" This morning, Lieutenant Wong placed himself at my disposal. Finding that there were no duties that would detain me upon shipboard, I told the Lieutenant that I desired to visit friends on shore. We proceeded at once to Marlborough street. The door of the Nesmyth's house was opened by Margaretta herself who gave a scream of joy at seeing me, and greeted me most affectionately. She blushed furiously, however, when she saw that her rapture had been observed by my Chinese companion, and then suddenly grew so pale that for a moment I thought she was going to faint. I learned afterward that her first thought had been that I was under arrest. She soon perceived her error, however, and I speedily introduced Lieutenant Wong, who, upon Mrs. Nesmyth's appearance, proceeded with fine tact to make himself agreeable to the elder lady.

" Edith and I had much to talk about. She insisted on my

telling her the details of our flight to Chicago, and this consumed some time. Indeed, before I had finished, the luncheon hour arrived, and as neither Mrs. Nesmyth nor Margaretta would hear of our leaving, Lieutenant Wong and I stayed to luncheon.

" After luncheon Lieutenant Wong proposed that he should take his departure, humorously suggesting that in his native land they had a proverb to the effect that 'the third bird in the nest is often, in the way.' He left us, therefore, after cautioning me of the inadvisability of my leaving the house until his return which, at Mrs. Nesmyth's suggestion, he agreed would be at dinner time. Margaretta assured him that she would not let me depart until he came.

" Left thus alone we could talk more freely, and as I had spent the morning in telling my experience I insisted upon Margaretta's using the afternoon to tell me hers. She gave me a very graphic account of poor Jack Storiot's death. He was one of those who had been assembled on the Common for deportation, and one of the first whom it had been attempted to manacle. We all knew Jack's high spirit and impetuosity, and I have no doubt that this insult of the Chinese threw him into a great passion. He was one of the first to attack the Chinese soldiers and fell most horribly mutilated. Margaretta told me that one of the papers had published a list of those who had been killed or wounded in this horrible massacre. The paper had been suppressed by the Chinese as soon as it appeared, but the Nesmyth's had fortunately been able to secure a copy, and this she now brought to me.

" As I read over the list of names I saw many that I knew; fortunately, my intimate friends had not been there, but Tom Hammond, Lafayette Brett, Babcock Tyler and Will Peckham were mong the killed, and Aleck Warner, Charlie Bell and several other old school friends were among the wounded. It was an awful thing, I spoke of it that evening to Commissioner Hi and he told me that no one could regret it more than the Chinese did. It was one of the terrible results of war, to be excused only by its necessity. 'We have hearts,' he said, "but we must do our duty.'

" Then Margaretta told me some of the discomforts that had come to her own family, though I think the dear girl hid many from me and made light of others for fear of too greatly giving me pain. She told me how the Chinese had taken possession of the ward eating-houses, and how still later, their credit cards had lost their purchasing power. She gave me a graphic picture of how by selling to the Chinese the pictures and most valuable ornaments of the house, they had procured a supply of new credit cards, or as they were called, 'paper moneys.' Her mother, she said, had sold all her jewelry, and her father had parted with his gold watch; and then very shyly and with many blushes, she called my attention to the fact that she no longer wore the engagement ring I had given her. I asked her why and she confessed that she had sold it.

" 'Sold it !' I exclaimed, in wonderment.

"' Yes,' she said. ' I sold it. You are not angry are you ? I sold it to the Chinese and they gave me $500 for it.'

" 'About half its value,' I thought, for I remembered that I had swopped a very rare vase (that grandfather had given me) for it, with Peter Kyon, whose aunt had left this ring to him by her will.

"' Of course I am not angry with you, my dear, I said, ' but I should like to know why you sold it ? Is it possible that you were so ' poor' (I think that is what it is called) that you had to part with it to procure the necessities of life ?'

" * Oh, no!' she said, hastily. ' So far we have always been able to get nearly every thing we have wanted. But there have been a great many people who have not been as fortunate as we have, because after their credit cards became valueless, they had little of any value to get the Chinese money with, and you know that Chinese money is the only thing anybody can buy any thing with now !'

" I said I hadn't thought of that before; and then I asked Margaretta how she had spent the money. She said that there had been so many people who suffered because they could not buy things, that the people of Boston had formed societies to relieve the sufferings of those who were now designated by the word ' poor.' (Margaretta thought this was a new word, but I told her I was quite sure that I had heard father use it as applying to a class of people who existed when he was young.) These societies, she said, were modelled after certain societies of the nineteenth century, and were called ' King's Daughters'— though why I don't know, as there is no 'King' outside of China, and he is called an 'Emperor.' I must remember to ask about this. She said that the society to which she belonged, had promised to take care of all the 'poor' people in their ward, and that she had sold her engagement ring that this society might be able to buy food for those who could not buy it themselves.

'"I hope you are not very angry with me?' she said, as she finished telling me why she had parted with my gift.

"' I will forgive you,' I answered, 'if you will give me a kiss !'

" She kissed me twice, and then I, to show her that I was not offended, kissed her more than twice. Then I promised her that I would speak to father and ask him if he could remember any thing about these societies.

" She told me then that one of the things that had led to the formation of these societies had been the robbery of the Bassett and Hayes houses. I had not heard of this, so I begged her to tell me about it. She said that after the Chinese had taken possession of the ward eating-houses and refused to sell things for credit, or on the presentation of credit cards, a great many people found themselves unable to procure food, having nothing that the Chinese would give them money for. Quite a number of these people, rendered desperate by their hunger, and acting probably at the instigation of the Chinese, one night, about twelve o'clock, entered the Bassetts house and removed from it all those pictures which the Bassetts had been collecting for many years. These pictures were at once taken to the place which the Chinese had established for the sale of valuables, and which was called 'The Bank,' and the money paid for them was distributed among the thieves. An hour later, Mr. Hayes' house was visited in like manner, and the family were forced to give up whatever jewels they possessed. Mr. Hayes, Margaretta said, was nearly beaten to death, before he could be made to disclose where most of the jewels were kept.

" We were still talking, regardless of time, when the arrival of Lieutenant Wong warned us that it must be near the dinner hour. Mr. Nesmyth came in shortly afterward, and half an hour later we were seated at the dinner table.

"We said good-night to the Nesmyths, about half-past eight, as Lieutenant Wong told me that the Admiral would probably expect me to call upon him that evening. I promised Margaretta to see her, if possible, some time the next day.

" The Admiral was entertaining father and some of the officers of the fleet, and I stayed in his cabin until about eleven o'clock. After I had taken my leave, and was going to my stateroom (which was next to Lieutenant Wong's), Wong called to me, telling me that if I was not sleepy, to come in and smoke a cigar with him. As I felt no inclination to go to bed, I accepted his invitation, and we fell to chatting about Boston. He told me that most of the Chinese officers were interestied in Nationalism, but that though they understood its theory, they knew little of its practical working. Being now looked upon as enemies, there was no social intercourse between them and the Bostonians; to-day had been the first time, he said, that he had been inside a Boston gentleman's house.

" I gave him an account of how I had spent my own life, told him about our guild yacht races, ball clubs, and so forth, and tried to explain to him what I had expected the rest of my life to be like. Then, changing the subject, I asked him if it would be possible for me to get a diamond ring.

"' A diamond ring!' he said, with polite surprise, for my question, being in no way related to what we had been talking about, was no doubt exceedingly abrupt. ' I suppose you could,' he added, ' but I don't know exactly where. I am afraid we are buying, not selling, those things.'

" I told him, then, how Miss Nesmyth had sold her engagement ring, and that I wished to give her another in the place of the one disposed of.

" He thought a few minutes, then he said, 'I don't know exactly how our purchases of such things are arranged, but I think that there must be a record kept of such purchases; indeed there must be, for somebody will have to give an account of the money that is issued. If you will find out on what day and at what place Miss Nesmyth sold her ring, I'll see if I can't get it back for you.'

"Of course it would be much nicer if I could give Margaretta the identical ring I had given her before, and I promised to try and find out from her where and when she had sold it. The next morning I spoke to father about it. He said he had no objection to my doing as I wished, but asked me how I intended to pay for it — what I intended to give in exchange for it. I told him that grandfather had left me a picture by Coxe, and that if he had no objection, I might be able to use that. He asked me where that picture was.

" ' "Why, it's at home, of course,' I said. ' Don't you remember that it was hanging on the parlor wall ? It must be worth more than $500.'

"' My dear boy,' said my father, ' our house is ours no longer. It, and all that we left in it, belongs to the Chinese. Your picture has long ago been confiscated. Even if the Chinese were willing to give you this picture, or even the ring you want, you could not accept either, as it would be improper for you, holding, as you do now, a public position, to accept presents from them. You must think of something else.'

" I was terribly disappointed. Except what I had had at home, I had nothing to offer in exchange.

" ' I think I can help you,' said my father, as he say my disappointment. ' The stone was a valuable one, and it is not likely that diamonds will ever lose very much of their value. Suppose we try what some of the gold we have about us will do.'

" ' Why, yes,' I said, ' it might be quite a curiosity to some of the Chinese, but do you suppose that what we have will be sufficiently curious to buy a $500 ring?'

" ' We have between us,' said my father, 'about $3,000 in gold coin. A Chinese tael is equivalent to a dollar and a half — at least that has been the estimate of its value in the negotiations, for the city's ransom. Now, if one dollar and a half is worth one tael, how many taels are $3,000 worth.'

" ' Two thousand taels,' I answered.

" 'Well,' said father, 'I don't suppose our gold is worthless because it has been minted by the United States. No doubt the Chinese would value our double eagles at $20. But in this case you had better leave the changing of our money to me, Leete. If you can find out where the ring is and how many taels it can be bought for, then come to me and I will see if we cannot get our American gold changed for Chinese money.

" I visited Margaretta that morning, and managed, without raising her suspicious to get her to mention where and when she had sold the ring. Then after leaving her. Lieutenant Wong and I went to the place. The Lieutenant had no trouble in obtaining the information we wanted. Upon his giving his name and rank we were at once ushered into the room of the Superintendent of the Bank. I was introduced and my errand made known. A short conversation then followed between Wong and the Superintendent which ended in the latter's ringing a bell and giving some order in Chinese to the person who answered. In a few minutes a book was brought in and opened at a certain page, and I was requested to look through this and the succeeding pages and point out Miss Nesmyth's signature. This I was quickly able to do, whereupon the Superintendent returned the book to its bearer and gave him some other order. We waited now about half an hour during which the Superintendent explained to us the system of the Bank.

" Whatever was offered was appraised by one of several appraisers, goods of a certain class by one appraiser, goods of another by another appraiser, and so on. ; The thing offered was then numbered, a short description of it written in a book and numbered the same as the article, and a receipt, likewise numbered, signed by the person who received pay for it. The article was then taken and placed in a storehouse and if subsequently sold, that fact was noted and the name of the purchaser recorded under the same number. Thus by knowing the number of a thing, its whole history while in possession of the Chinese could be at once known.

" At the expiration of the half hour a clerk appeared and handed the ring to the Superintendent, who passed it to me, asking if it was the one I wished. I told him it was, and pointed Margaretta's and my own initials engraved on the inner surface. He said that it had not been sold, but still remained the property of the Chinese government and that he would very willing sell it to me for the price that had been paid for, namely, $500. I asked him if he would keep it for me until to-morrow, as I had not now so much money with me, and he consented at once.

" Father bought it for me the next day and I surprised Margaretta very much by presenting her with it."

## Chapter 13 LECTURE XIII.

Before resuming my quotations from the manuscript account of Leete "West's experiences while in Boston, I invite your attention to a subject of which that manuscript does not treat. I mean the very general impoverishment that followed the Chinese invasion, and which was accelerated by the formation of charitable societies such as the one referred to in my last lecture.

The longer the Chinese stayed in Boston, the poorer the inhabitants of that city became. Those who were numbered among the workers received a salary or wage which as least kept them from starvation, but those who did not so work — and these included all the children and all persons over forty-five years of age — received nothing, and were obliged to live on what property they had chanced to accumulate. As nearly every one had some such property, it was supposed by the Chinese statesmen that it would be some time before absolute poverty and penury became very general. They reasoned that a person who found himself with only $100 of money, and with no expectation of receiving more, would naturally be as economical as possible, and endeavor to make that money last as long as they could. This was one of the few instances in which the reasoning of our statesmen was wrong. The majority of the Bostonians did not economise, but (owing to various circumstances) spent, generally, more than they would have spent had the Chinese invasion never have happened.

Let us look at the reasons for this. For at least three generations there had been no necessity for any person to lay up money or things upon which to subsist in time of sickness or of old age. Such provident habits were, indeed, discouraged by the

Nationalists, when, at the end of each year, the amount unspent upon the credit card became worthless. Up to the time when Nationalism had been adopted by the United States, the American people, though by no means lacking in forethought, were in no manner distinguished, as a race, for frugality. There was no racial predisposition toward provident habits, but, indeed, rather the reverse, and the effect of the Nationalistic theory upon this national characteristic, was to make the race less and less provident and saving.

Thus, those Bostonians who received money for goods, had neither experience nor a racial instinct to prompt them to economy. The young people had the generosity of youth, the old had the habit of a lifetime which unconsciously prompted them to think that the money they how possessed would somehow or other lose its value (as the credit card would have) at the end of the year, when, as there always had been a new supply forthcoming, there must be a new supply again.

In addition, for the first time in three generations, there came to them the demands of charity, which they met with the impulsive generosity of children who had just received pocket-money. The Chinese invasion inaugurated among the citizens of the coast cities, not an era of economy, but rather an era of extravagance.

I return now to the manuscript from which I quoted in my last lecture.

" Two days before we were to return to Albany, I received a summons to attend the Admiral in his cabin.

"' Mr. West, said he, after his first greetings had passed, ' your father and I have had some conversation on a topic on which you naturally feel great interest. I mean your marriage.'

" I looked at him with astonishment, and did not know what to say, but he saved me the necessity ot replying, by continuing:

" You retum to Albany in two days. I have mentioned to your father, and I will now say to you (in strict confidence, however) that every one of the demands of the Nationalist Commissioners will be refused. Our gracious Emperor has instructed us to accept no terms, except an absolute and unconditional surrender of the entire territory of the United States. I rely upon you not to mention this until after it has been made public by your Congress.'

" Of course, I at once gave the necessary promise, and he went on:

"' Under these circumstances, you will, of course, not wish to return to Boston, where you will be hourly in danger of deportation, but I can imagine that you would be equally unwilling to leave your lady-love in the territory of the enemy. I cannot wisely give Miss Nesmyth leave to depart, as it would be establishing a precedent that would prove extremely inconvenient, and subject me personally to the charge of favoritism. But,' he added with a smile, 'if you can arrange any way in which the young lady can smuggle herself upon the train by which you return, I think I can promise you that as long as she remains in hiding she will be invisible to the officials. The suggestion also includes her father and mother, if you so desire.'

" I thanked the Admiral heartily, as may be supposed, and said that I would at once advise with Miss Nesmyth.

" ' It is necessary, I suppose, that you should do so,' answered the Admiral. ' But mind, Mr. West, not a word or a hint in public of what I told you; nor must any one except I and you, and the person I shall shortly introduce you to, ever have the slightest knowledge that I am acquainted with the intention of Miss Nesmyth to escape. I will introduce you to Lieutenant Foo, who will have charge of your train. You must lead the young lady to suppose that you have made your arrangements with him alone; but you must impress upon her the necessity of absolute secrecy, if such a thing be possible to a woman, and inform her that the slightest whisper of her intention to leave town will remove the blindness from official eyes. You will not speak of this matter again to me, but arrange all the details with Lieutenant Foo.'

" He touched a bell and bade the sentry call Lieutenant Foo. That gentleman entered immediately; he evidently had been waiting outside, and the Admiral introduced us to each other. Then by a happily worded wish that my married life might be happy, he signified that my audience was concluded.

" We left the Admiral's cabin, and in a single sentence, Lieutenant Foo gave me notice that he was already thoroughly familiar with the object in view.

" ' You will probably wish,' he said, ' to see the young lady at once. If that be the case, you will find Lieutenant Wong in his stateroom. 'It is preferable that he receive no notification of what is intended, though,' and he looked at me with a meaning smile, 'his eyesight and hearing have been greatly impaired of late.'

" My first impulse was to go at once to Margaretta, but almost instantly I decided otherwise.

" ' Would it not be better,' I said to Lieutenant Foo, ' if you and I were to devise some plan and not mention it to the ladies until the time for departure comes ?'

"' Much better,' he answered. ' If you will come to my office we will talk over the matter at once.'

" Leaving me alone for a moment, he stepped into Lieutenant Wong's room and said a word or two to him — announcing probably that he would be my escort—then asking me to precede him, we went over the side of the ship, and to his office which was near the railway yards.

" He showed me the diagram of the car which we were to travel in. It was the car built for the Superintendent of the Eastern Railroad division. There was a large stateroom and dressing-room at either end, and the space between was arranged as a drawing-room.

" ' One stateroom has been allotted to you and the other to your father,' he said. ' The train will consist of four passenger cars. The first two will be for Commissioner Hi and his suite, then will come your car, my own car will be the last. You will thus be between Commissioner Hi's car and my own, and no one will be permitted to pass through your car without, notice being given. If your father should be ill, it will afford an excuse to keep the greater portion of the curtains drawn, and to prevent the passage of persons through the car.'

"'Does my fathier know of the plan?' I asked.

"'He must not know of it,' he replied. 'It would never do for a Commissioner of the United States to connive at prisoners escaping in his car.'

"'But how can we hide the fact from him?' I asked.

"'I have a suspicion,' said Lieutenant Foo, with a twinkle in his eye, 'that your father will enter the car by the door nearest his room, so ill that he will at once retire and remain ill and confined to his room until Albany is reached.'

"I smiled, for I saw at once the purpose of my father's illness.

"'Now,' I said,' where shall our friends hide—in my stateroom, I suppose, while Mr. Nesmyth and I sleep on the lounges in the drawing-room?'

"'The ladies can occupy the room, but the gentleman must sleep in the dressing-room. It would be too great a risk to allow him to sleep elsewhere. I must ask you, also, to see that they leave the stateroom as little as possible and keep the doors locked.'

"' How shall we get them there ?' I asked.

" ' That is the most difficult matter of all,' he replied. ' We must either smuggle them in the night before, which will be difficult; or better yet, if they will consent, I can obtain a blank requisition for a man and two women to clean the car, and they can present it, filled out in their names, to me and thus disarm all notice or suspicion. Once in the car they must either make a pretense of working for a while, or at once conceal themselves — which, I must judge of at the time ; but I shall be able to inform them when they arrive.'

" 'They will have to take some baggage with them,' I remarked.

" 'They must come empty-handed, of course,' said Lieutenant Foo. ' But if they wish to send a couple of trunks of clothing, and so forth, to your mother and sisters, I see no reason why you have not a perfect right to take it. But do not make them more than two. I must ask you also to see that in one of the trunks there is food enough to last for four or five days, as I shall not be able to supply you with more food than you could reasonably be supposed to eat yourself. Your father, being ill, will have a light appetite, and may, perhaps, refuse his meals once or twice; it would, therefore, be no harm for you to have a few delicacies, such as potted meats, etc., to tempt his appetite. I could put two small trnnks in your car, as a matter of course, but more might excite comment.'

" 'And when we arrive at Albany, what then ?' I queried.

" ' I have arranged for that. The Admiral has received a written request from Mr. Robert Goodale, the Assistant Chief of your Railroad Department at Chicago, to forward this car to him, and has decided to comply with the request, although he has written to say that the request is a very unusual one, and must not be construed as a precedent. As soon, therefore, as you and your father debark at Albany, I shall myself take the car to Chicago and hand it over to Mr. Robert Goodale, with the Admiral's letter. I should say that provisions for six days would be enough, and I shall be very glad to oblige you by taking charge of the trunks you destine for your mother, and seeing them safely into her hands.'

"' It is a very fortunate coincidence,' said I, * that Mr. Goodale should apply for this car just at this time, isn't it ?'

" ' Very !' he responded, smiling.

" I understood the meaning of that smile better when I learned later that upon Lieutenant Foo's arrival in Chicago, Mr. Goodale indignantly repudiated the letter as a forgery and at once returned the car to the Admiral.

" 'Now,' said Lieutenant Foo, 'I suppose you will want to see your friends. In that case, we had better return to the ship, where you will probably find Wong waiting for you.'

" I lunched with the officers on board the man-of-war ; then, accompanied by Lieutenant Wong, I went to the Nesmyths. As soon as we had entered, Wong said that he had some papers to read, and requested that he might be permitted to retire to a private room. He was shown to the sitting-room upstairs, and Margaretta, who had taken quite a fancy to him— which I laughingly told her, almost made me jealous—sent up to him a decanter of madeira and a box of her father's best cigars. We then returned to the parlor, her mother, at my request, accompanying us.

" We had no sooner seated ourselves than the door opened and Mr. Nesmyth walked in. We were all surprised to see him, far it was much earlier than his usual hour for returning from work. His wife was quite fearful that he was ill.

"'No,' he said in answer to our inquiries, 'I'm not ill. I wish that was all that was the matter with me. I have been dismissed from the industrial service, that is all. Dismissed before my time of labor has expired. Dismissed without any reason being given, except that my services were no longer required. Dismissed without cause, without any opportunity given me to meet any charges against me. It is a most high-handed, outrageous proceeding. As a man who has always done his duty well and conscientiously, I am free to say that better treatment was due to me. The Chinese boast that they have a consideration for a man because of his ancestry, and tell us we are barbarians because we look only to a man's personal and individual worth; and I had thought that, therefore, they might have some consideration for me as the representative of one of the most ancient families of Boston. But, of course, I was mistaken. They are not men, they are brutes in human form. Cruel, vindictive and unscrupulous. They know nothing of moral principle, the rights of man, the dictates of justice.'

" He was very angry," his pride was severely hurt; for under the Nationalistic theory, no man could be dismissed from the industrial force without good cause and after a fair and impartial trial; and a dismissal was the worst disgrace that could be put upon a person. It made him a social pariah, with whom no one would associate. He was very angry and he indulged in a bitter tirade. But I confess, that as soon as I recovered from the first shock of the news, I found myself wondering if this were an accidental or a purposely contrived coincidence. The more I considered, the more I detected a purpose in it.

"I waited until the first vehemence of Mr. Nesmyth's passion had subsided. Then I begged his permission to say a word. I told him I thought I knew why he had been dismissed, and then, in answer to the eager inquiries of all, I said that Lieutenant Foo would have charge of the train that father and I would return on, and that I had arranged with him that they could go with us. Then, I explained to them the method that had been devised for their escape. I dissimulated far enough to let them think that Lieutenant Foo was the only person privy to their flight; and I impressed upon them the necessity of absolute secrecy.

" 'I think,' I then said to Mr. Nesmyth, 'that if we could ever know the real truth of this matter, we would find that your dismissal had been purposely arranged so that theie might be no insinuation that you had deserted from your post.'

" ' It may be so,' said Mr. Nesmyth, ' but in attempting to do me that service, he has subjected me to a great disgrace.'

" 'I cannot see it in that light,' I ventured to reply. 'You were not lawfully dismissed. You were dismissed by our enemies, our invaders. Your dismissal is effective only because the arms of the Chinese make it so.'

" ' Then if I am not lawfully dismissed it is my duty to remain at my post,' said Mr. Nesmyth.

" Margaretta and her mother looked very blank at this, and I hastened to reply.

" ' I don't think so,' I said. ' You have been ousted from your position by force, by force used by our enemies. It seems to me that it is your duty to proceed at once to the central government and report the fact to them. The Chinese will not permit you to leave openly. You must leave secretly. And, unless you have some better plan to propose, I see no way for you to get to Chicago than by that which I have just proposed to you.'

" I had expected that whatever objections would be made to the plan of flight would come from the ladies; but the unexpected turn of events, by involving Mr. Nesmyth's safety, had made Margaretta and her mother careless of all considerations affecting their own comfort, and they now joined me in entreating Mr. Nesmyth to give his approval to the plan that had been made. Finally he consented.

" All this had taken some time, and it was now growing dark. I hastened to Lieutenant Wong.

" He smiled at my apologies for leaving him so long solitary, said that he was in no hurry to return, and handed me a letter which he said Lieutenant Foo had requested him to give to me. It inclosed the blank requisition or order which I have already mentioned. The letter requested me to fill this up with the names of any friends who might be in need of employment, and to bid the persons be in the yard at nine o' clock. My train, it said, would leave at eleven, and suggested that, as I would probably not be able to visit the city after that evening, it might be well to take final leave of Miss Nesmyth and all other personal friends before returning to the ship — the trunks I had spoken of would be called for, at any place designated by me at half past seven the next morning.

" I went down stairs and showed this letter to the Nesmyths, and filling in the blank order with their names gave it to Margaretta's father; then, that gentleman went out and arranged that dinner should be sent in from the ward eating-house, Lieutenant Wong was invited to come down stairs and we all dined quite merrily. We left about nine o'clock.

" The parting between Margaretta and myself was very sad. We were left alone in the hall for a few minutes, and both of us knew that should our plans miscarry, we might never meet again. She threw her arms around my neck and cried, while I, myself, feeling as if I too would shed tears, could only comfort her with kisses. At last I tore myself away and went with Wong back to my quarters on shipboard."

I have quoted thus at length from this manuscript, because the episode which it narrates shows that the Chinese officers, to whom was confided the task of conquering, had tender and sympathetic hearts.

It has been the fashion, in Nationalistic circles to abuse the Chinese, to call them devils, monsters and ogres, and to impute to them horrible and diabolic motives. This is not right. As men, they were courteous and hospitable and kind. As servants of our gracious Emperor, they had duties to peform, some of which were necessarily distasteful to their humane hearts. They regarded, as all our statesmen did, the Chinafication of the United States, as a moral duty we owed our own nation, which otherwise might have been tainted with the Nationalism, which most of the world had been infected with. They had hearts. They shed many tears over the sufferings of the captive nation.

That they may be judged less harshly, is my excuse for quoting at such length from this manuscript.

Note — For the benefit of those who may have become interested in the plight, of the Nesmyths, the Editor begs to say that they escaped in safety to Chicago, the plan devised by Lieutenant Foo being entirely successful. The Nationalist authorities approved of Mr. Nesmyth's departure from Boston, and at once reinstated him to his former rank in the industrial army. He is now an officer of the military branch of the service.

The marriage of Leete West and Margaretta Nesmyth took place early in the following spring.

*Chapter 14 LECTURE XIV.*

It is with regret that I cease to quote from Professor West's diary. I trust that during your next year's course of historical study you will have the opportunity of perusing it in its entirety. Though bearing marks of evident haste, though often fragmentary and disconnected, it is valuable as a contemporary narrative of events, and invaluable for the comparisons which Professor West makes, of the workings of the governments of the nineteenth and twenty-first centuries.

What I have to say to you to-day, in this, the closing lecture of your freshman year, will be expressed to you in my own words.

On the reassembling of the Commissioners at Albany, the Chinese Commissioners gave a categorical refusal to each of the demands of the Nationalists, and made a general demand for the surrender of the Nation. The American Commissioners, therefore, returned to Chicago having accomplished nothing except so far as their observations in the cities they had visited might be of value.

Congress was in session when they returned and then, for the first time, active measures were taken for resistance. The firearms that had been captured at West Point had arrived, and orders had been given for their reproduction. Steps had been taken to form armies. A committee of Congress with the President at its head had been placed in charge of the conduct of the war.

It must be admitted that the steps taken by Congress were the best that could be taken under the circumstances, but time is a necessary factor in preparations for war — and time is unaffected by the enactments of legislatures.

In all these measures Professor Julian West took an active part. He became the colonel of the regiment raised from among the students of Shawmut College who had escaped from the territory held by the Chinese, and was subsequently promoted to be General of the brigade into which all the college regiments were collected. He fell on the 6th of August, 2022, while leading his old regiment at what is generally known as the battle of Lake Erie, but which should more properly be styled the second battle of Lake Erie, to distinguish it from one of the most gallant events in the world's history — the battle fought on the 10th of September, 1813, and won by the skill and personal bravery of Ohver Hazard Perry.

As your previous studies have acquainted you with the various battles and warlike movements which took place after the Nationalists had become fairly aroused to the gravity of their situation I shall not now consume time by narrating them, but pass at once to a hasty summary of the doings of the Chinese.

The general policy of the Chinese had been matured, some time before the declaration of war, by the principal state officers of China, and had been imparted to the Admirals of the several fleets before they had departed from the Celestial Kingdom.

It was to subjugate the country by numbers, rather than to attempt to hold possession of it by armies. "We recognized that while a population, as numerous and skillful as the Americans were, might be captured by a sudden surprise, it would be yet merely a question of time before they recovered from their surprise, and rose against the invaders. If the United States was to be held by China, then the people of the United

States must be willing subjects of China—or, at least, such a majority of the people as to render all attempts at resistance individual, and not National.

In pursuance of this policy, every man, woman and child, who could be spared from China, was to be shipped to America, as soon as the seaport towns were captured. It was deemed wise at first, to change the form and system of government as little as possible, and to allow the people to see as little difference as possible between the old order and the new, and to rule them as far as could be, in the same way that they had been always ruled. By acting thus it was supposed that the risks of rebellion would be greatly reduced — that the Americans, being dominated with the aspiration for material prosperity, would care little who ruled them as long as this remained. Hence the ranks of the laborers were to be kept in numbers as nearly as possible what they were before.

The deportation of Americans was a logical outgrowth of this policy. Every American deported was one less enemy to fight, while at the same time the place that he had filled was opened to a Chinese. As soon as any number of Chinese became domiciled in any locality the influence of their opinion would produce results tending to still further solidify the hold of China upon the country — woman, who had been most unduly exalted, under the Nationalistic idea, to an equality with man, would sink to the proper state of subordination, and then another element of danger would be eliminated, and another opening made for Chinese labor. China could pour one hundred million of people into the United States and be none the poorer—nay, indeed, she would be enriched thereby. A fertile land would become tributary to her, and her surplus population would find a safe outlet. There was no fear that her expatriated people would become less loyal subjects of her Emperors. The desire possessed by every Chinaman, high or low in estate, rich or poor in this world's goods, is that his dust may repose in the soil of China, and the history of the race has shown that this desire is sufficient to prevent the absent sons of China from becoming other than transient citizens of foreign lands.

While the armed hordes of the Chinese were to march from the sea-coast to the interior, following the courses of the rivers and the natural highways of commerce, and gradually drawing an impenetrable ring, closer and closer around whatever Nationalistic government might exist in the interior of the country, they were to leave behind them no hostile country, but a land which was largely peopled with Chinese, and which gave a willing fealty to China.

This was the general policy which the Admirals of the fleets were to follow until such time as a sufficient space of country had been conquered, when a special Governor of such territory was to be appointed.

The ways in which the different Admirals carried out their instructions were much alike, although not wholly the same. The action of Admiral Sing, who took possession of Boston, may be, however, considered as generally representative of the methods everywhere displayed.

When Boston was seized, the first points taken possession of were the Munieipal Council-House and the Central Warehouse. The machinery of government and the supply of food, clothing and other necessities of life came thus at once into our possession. The Municipal Councillors, though prisoners, were at first permitted to govern the city in the usual way, care being taken that they did nothing to create rebellion. The orders from the sample houses were received and distributed as before from the central warehouses. As the numbers of the Chinese increased, however, officers of the Chinese government became members of the Municipal Council, removable only at the pleasure of the Governor or Admiral. In the same way the native Superintendents, were replaced by or placed under the direct supervision of native Chinese. The changes being, as far as possible, restricted to the personnel of the rulers, and there being no radical change in the form of government, there was little to remind the populace of their subjugation.

A populace seldom stops long to reason on abstract subjects. Feed it, clothe it, keep it at work and now and then amused, house it decently, and it will remain pacified and content. It cares little who its rulers may be so long as its personal well-being is assured. Only when its stomach is empty, its clothes ragged, and when wealth flaunts before its face a glaring inequality between the rich and the poor, does it growl and grumble and become turbulent and rebellious.

The question of the credit cards was one that for a time offered many perplexities. They were the symbols of wealth, and wealth without production to support it is an element of weakness, as is also too great an inequality in its distribution. Far back in the nineteenth century, as long ago as 1837, a high authority, John C. Calhoun, said in the Senate, " It is the remark of a profound statesman, that the revenue is the State, and that of course those who control the revenue control the State; and those who can control the money power can control the revenue, and through it the State with the property and industry of the country in all its ramifications."

It was impossible for the Chinese to recognize permanently the credit cards of the Nationalists and to continue to part with yards of cloth and pounds of meat and flour, receiving therefor only worthless bits of punched paper. It was equally impossible to cut off all supplies from the citizens without creating riots of the worst kind. There was no money to afford a circulating medium, and if there had been, the problem of its distribution would have still remained.

The difficulty was met as follows: The credit cards of the Nationalists were declared worthless; paper money of various denommations was printed by the Chinese, and a regular sum of this was paid at stated intervals to each worker — all native American workers receiving equal sums, while the wages of Chinese workers were graded. Those who were not workers, however, received nothing of this allowance. Children were obliged to rely upon their parents for support. Elderly people who had passed forty-five, and who, under the Nationalistic system, had been idlers, were entirely excluded from this distribution.

To prevent, however, any disturbances arising from so large a class of the community being without the means of purchasing food, a bureau was opened in the central portion of the city where any citizen could take such valuables as they possessed. Chinese assessors were appointed to remain at this station, and to value all goods and chattels there presented ; and the value thus appraised, was given in paper money to the owner. In this way most of the property of the citizens came in time to be the property of the invaders.

Naturally, under this system, those who had accumulated many valuables, either by inheritance or through the spirit of acquisitiveness, fared better than those who had little to sell; and the family few in numbers was better off than a larger one. These inequalities provoked envies and jealousies which undermined the fraternal feeling which had prevailed under the Nationalistic government, and tended to hinder any combined resistance on the part of the natives. The curious custom, which the Bostonians of that day had inherited from their ancestors, of but slightly protecting their dwellings by fastenings, resulted in many robberies, which increased the distance between the poor and the rich.

That this policy was the wisest that could have been devised is shown by the fact that it was put into practice with great ease and with scarcely any opposition from the people. Discontent must, to some extent, have followed any system substituted for the former one, but as I have abeady shown you, this discontent was directed against classes of native Americans, rather than against the Chinese.

While all Chinese statesmen have admitted the astonishing success of this policy of reforming the government of the subjugated territory, there is by no means a similar unanimity of opinion about the ability with which the military conquest was prosecuted. It has been argued that there was nothing to prevent the Chinese armies from traversing the continent from one end to the other, except the possibility that the Nationalists might have, in that event, retarded our passage by destroying the railroads. This, however, it is said, there was little probability of their doing, since under the Nationalistic theory each part of the country had become so dependent upon each other part that so serious an obstruction to the distribution of products would have infallibly broken the Nationalistic government itself into fragments—the step, it is argued, would have been political *hari-kari.*

The advantages which might have resulted from such a rapid advance are purely conjectural, though the idea itself will probably be fruitful to the imagination of the future novelist. For myself, I have never been able to appreciate what practical advantage would have come from such a meteor-like flitting from one point to another, leaving no trace of permanent occupation behind.

You know the policy that was adopted. It was first of all to take possession of the principal coast cities, then, when the government of these had been thoroughly systemized and enough Chinese had been settled in and about them to make certain their permanent allegiance to the Celestial Kingdom, to advance to the nearest great cities of the interior and to remain there until all the country in the rear had been re-created into a Chinese province. The army was thus made the wall of a new civilization. It was strengthed by leaving behind it no hostile territory. The further it advanced the greater became the base of its supplies immediately behind it. Every foot of its progress was permanent.

At the time that I speak to you, the Nationalists are hemmed in on all sides, save for the frozen north, from communication with outside nations. The front line of our armies forms a semi-circle stretching from Montreal south along the western base of the Alleghanies to the Ohio, whence it curves, and dipping to the south reaches the easterly base of the Rocky Mountains, along which it runs far north of the latitude of Puget Sound. Behind this wall, whose bricks are armed men, is a thriving population wholly devoted to our Celestial Emperor.

If our progress has been slow, it has also been sure, and irresistible. It is but a question of time when we close in upon the last remnant of the Nationalists and the country be at peace. The conditions of our future advance will, however, differ from those of the past. The Nationalists have learned from their reverses, and the Nationalistic system of government has been changed until to-day it does not so much differ from that which we enjoy.

Let us now, in closing, consider hastily the benefits which the invasion of the Chinese has brought to us.

We are no longer a defenseless people, ready to to be subjugated by the first armed nation that attacks. Our material prosperity was never greater. Our soil supports a greater population than it did before. Chinese frugality has replaced the wasteful lavishness that prevailed in private life under the Nationalistic government. Woman no longer competes with man, but has become as the Gods intended she should be, the handmaiden of male humanity. What was good in Nationalism we have retained. What was bad we have discarded and replaced by what is better. Under Nationalism, individualism was reduced to a minimum; with us to-day it is honored and given every chance to develop.

THE END

Lightning Source UK Ltd.
Milton Keynes UK
UKHW022237220119
336029UK00009B/802/P